Rock'N'Roll in Locker Seventeen

SHANNON BROWN

This book is a work of fiction. Any resemblance to actual events locales or persons, is entirely coincidental.

DEDICATION

This book is for my Mom
Thanks for all the help and support

Prologue
Pacific Palisades, California, 1964

"Oh my God, he's gone, He's really gone," Jamie Underwood muttered, as he stood in the middle of the newly vacant living room. He hadn't given much thought to the note he discovered attached to his door earlier that morning, after all it wasn't as if Ricky Stevenson hadn't pulled stunts like this before.

Ricky and the Sleepers' latest album, *Drive Into the Sky* had finished six months behind schedule because most of the time when the band was supposed to be in the studio recording, the lead singer was two or more hours late or nowhere to be found. Jamie assumed Ricky was off living it up in Tijuana.

If any of the other members of the band tried to pull the shit that Ricky did they would be replaced in a second. Ricky Stevenson could get away with anything and he knew it. The fact that he never stuck around to greet the fans, or make any effort whatsoever to actually to promote their album only made him more popular.

Jamie, on the other hand, was always on time to the sessions, more than happy to sign autographs, and understood that you needed to tour to sell records and to keep your band in the consciousness of an ever fickle public; not that being a consummate professional meant anything in this business. All the executives at Emcee records cared about was whether or not you had a smile that could whip thousands of teenage girls into a manic frenzy. Jamie thought back to the album's review in *Musictime* magazine. Being named one of the best drummers in the business today was a great compliment, but in the end it didn't mean anything.

Jamie wandered upstairs and found Bobby and Carl standing in the middle of Ricky's bedroom. The carpet was darker beneath their feet and matted in the corners where Rickey's bedposts had been. The bed itself was gone along with every wall hanging and piece of furniture that wasn't built in.

"Whoever said you can't take it with you was wrong," Carl said. "Looks like Ricky decided to take our careers with him."

"Don't you have feelings, Carl?" Bobby responded. "He's dead, Ricky is probably at the bottom of some ravine and all you care about is the goddamn tour."

"He's not dead," Carl shrugged and turned to his other bandmate. "Hey Jamie, read me the part that says dear guys I am going to kill myself—'cause I must have missed that."

"Well he mentioned *Another Mississippi Morning* didn't he? Mentioning that song was a pretty big hint don't you think?" Bobby responded.

Jamie agreed with Bobby. The message had to be a suicide note, what else could it be, especially with that reference to *Another Mississippi Morning*. The melancholy song off of *The Palmdale Sessions* was never considered a favorite of Ricky and the Sleepers' largely young female fan base, probably because it's lyrics were about a young man who committed suicide by driving his truck off a bridge into the Mississippi River.

Jamie was overwhelmed by feelings of guilt. Why hadn't he been able to sense how depressed his friend was or once questioned Ricky's behavior? Jamie had barely given any thought to Ricky's frequent disappearing acts during the recording of *Drive into the Sky*; he simply attributed them to his friend's erratic personality. It never occurred to Jamie that Ricky Stevenson could actually be depressed. After all, he was the face of Ricky and the Sleepers. It was always Ricky who got the lion's share of attention. Be it at parties, in magazine interviews, and on television. It was always Ricky whose smile was plastered on the cover of whatever magazine had a story on the band that week while Jamie, Carl, and Bobby were relegated to pages inside. How in the world could you be despondent when everyone else's wildest dreams were constantly handed to you?

Jamie had gotten it all wrong. Instead of moaning about how his bandmate never had his priorities straight, he should have appreciated Ricky's friendship. Despite his fame and money, Ricky Stevenson had never stopped being a true Hollywood rarity; he was a decent guy and a genuine friend. So what if their lead singer didn't show up from time to time, all of Ricky and the Sleepers albums eventually got completed and went on to dominate the charts. If anything, Ricky's behavior seemed to be improving, he hadn't missed a single rehearsal in the past few weeks.

Jamie turned again to Carl and Bobby, who had poking through the emptied drawers of one of Ricky's built-in cabinets.

"What if Carl's right?" He said. "Maybe Ricky's not dead, and we can still find him. I mean he's one of the most famous people on the planet. It's not like he blends in. We've gotta make some calls, come on."

The three remaining members of Ricky and the Sleepers ran down the stairs and outside where they piled into Bobby's car. Everyone was suddenly in a hurry, but each had a sinking feeling they were already too late and would never see Ricky Stevenson again.

Chapter 1
Home of the Largest Lockers in Town

Delacourte, Indiana 30 Years Later

I was seventeen the year I made the discovery that would change my life forever. It all started the day I opened up the locker. I didn't technically have permission to open it but, I didn't really think I needed it. After all, the key wasn't supposed to work, and the door was definitely not supposed to run smoothly up is tracks like it did. The door was supposed to be broken and the space was supposed to be vacant. It wasn't.

...

It was late October and despite being a junior in high school, I still didn't have a girlfriend, or a car. I suspected there was a connection. Girls liked to be constantly taken places in style and a borrowed 1979 Cutlass Cruiser with the faded name of a storage franchise on the door is not exactly a chick magnet. What I did have was an after school job at the Delacourte, Indiana Stor'N'More self-storage franchise. Since the Stor'N'More e is attached to my house, I couldn't use the old--Mom, Dad I need a car so I can get to work-- excuse. So almost every day I spent my after school hours loading the outdated and always too heavy items of various residents of this city into one of the 235 usable spaces that make up our family business.

My boss happens to be my father, and if I ever decide to quit, Dad will make all my former duties as employee part of my unpaid chores. Despite his decision to pursue storage as a career, Jack R. White is not stupid. So I remained doomed to continue spending my days amongst this purgatory of cardboard, masking tape, and heavy-duty padlocks. I could always get out of a day of work if I told Dad I needed to study, but I needed the money, especially if I was ever going to get myself a halfway decent automobile.

My father's way of motivating me was to make me the permanent Stor'N'More employee of the month as soon as I started working for him. In order to assure the citizens of the greater Delacourte metropolitan area that Steven J. White is the best storage rental process coordinator this Stor'N'More has to offer, he used my little sister Jeanne's glue gun to festoon my embarrassing freshman yearbook photo upon a plaque that now sits on the office wall just beneath our Delacourte Area Chamber of Commerce membership. I tried to convince Dad that upping my official Stor'N'More paycheck was a far superior motivational tool than his foray into the world of arts and crafts, but he gave me a long-winded lecture about increasing competition in the local self-storage industry. I zoned off during most of this talk but I did notice that he used the phrase *lean Christmas* several times.

Our Stor'N'More is located in the southern end of Delacourte on Highland Avenue. While our town's northern end boasts tree-lined streets, a charming downtown, several parks and a well-known university, our closest neighbors consist of auto body shops, warehouses, and other light industry. When my father first purchased the Stor'N'More more than twenty years ago, we were one of the only businesses out this far. Since then, Highland has become one of the main thoroughfares through town. It makes its way toward the north and merges with Main just before downtown. This location may be good for visibility, but it leaves something to be desired when I have the need to concentrate on my homework, or when I have trouble getting to sleep. It's a wonder that I get any rest at all, since I also have to contend with the freight train that passes behind our place at regular intervals and the garish orange and blue neon Stor'N'More sign that spills light into my room, on a nightly basis.

We don't have a backyard, just acres of pavement stretched between 236 storage spaces of varying sizes. The only plant landscaping at the White homestead is a lone maple tree surrounded by a tiny patch of grass just by the gate and the motley assortment of weeds that grow along our back wall. Over the years when various teachers and others have discovered my address is on Highland, they have given me odd looks. I am sure they were picturing young Steven and his family living in a crowded apartment over Sal's Motorcycle Repair, or in a shed behind Jake's Roadside Bar and Grill. (Where you get twenty five percent off your meal, with proof of Hell's Angels membership.)

The truth is we live in a perfectly normal two story house on the Stor'N'More property. I am not sure why this has never occurred to most people, but when it comes to the family business, the average person is incredibly clueless.

Most people believe every storage space urban legend they have ever heard. According to my friends half of our storage spaces contain shipments of cocaine, mass amounts of gold bullion, and Jimmy Hoffa. The remaining spaces serve as housing for the entire homeless population of Delacourte. I don't know how people can believe someone could survive a harsh Indiana winter by staying in a dark un-insulated room with no electricity other than the lights overhead. How would you cook, where would you go to use the bathroom, and most importantly, how would you avoid detecting the almost sonar like ears of my father?

...

While most storage places in town have you sign a couple of papers before they hand you a padlock and say "have fun," the Stor'N'More chain goes that extra mile. If you purchase the deluxe package, you not only get the use of a genuine Stor'N'More handcart but loading and unloading assistance from its friendly helpful staff, which consists of Dad and me. Dad sometimes pays my little sister Jeanne to help us out, but she has elected not to become an official employee. Mom long ago got smart and got herself a job across town at the university so she wouldn't have to go near any dusty boxes, heavy doors, and cranky customers who can't remember their combination to open the gate.

Since personal storage is a very cyclical industry, hardly anyone ever rents a space in the fall and winter months. Once the snow hits, we may as well hightail it to the Bahamas for a couple of months because no one is in the mood to pay their belongings a holiday visit (they are too busy buying more stuff that will someday end up here). Things really begin to pick up for us in spring after the weather clears. Since our town is home to Delacourte University, locals know to rent a space long before the beginning of summer. On any typical spring Saturday you will see people loading and unloading old lawnmowers, hazardous looking toys, useless tools, exercise equipment, ugly clothes, and just about any item from old infomercials.

Every year without fail we fill every locker from May until August thanks to students loading up the furniture they had in their off campus apartments while they go home for the summer. I don't mind the college crowd because they are usually too cheap to opt for the deluxe package. I usually get to remain inside our nice air conditioned office like an employee at a normal storage place, while they load up secondhand coffee tables, cinderblock bookcases, stained couches, electric beer signs, rolled up nudie posters, and keg taps.

Aside from the students, the Stor'N'More gets a diverse clientele of permanent Delacourte residents. We tend to get a lot of small business owners, couples who are going through a divorce, and families about to move. The families are my least favorite Stor'N'More patrons, because they almost never pay for the deluxe package but Dad and I usually end up helping them out anyway.

The only locker that always remains empty is number seventeen. When my father bought the Stor'N'More, the doors originally came with their own locks, which became a pain because customers always lost the keys. Number seventeen's lock was missing its key and the door had a huge dent in it. According to Dad, there is no way the door will ever open because of this damage. When we switched to padlocks number seventeen's lock just would not come off and the door didn't seem salvageable. Dad now keeps a Coke machine in front of the dent so the renters can't see it. I highly doubt that most people who rent here would care that one of the lockers is damaged, considering the stuff they actually store, but every time I press the issue and suggest that we renovate the space, I am met with a glare and an explanation of the hundreds of more important little things that need doing around here. Most of these little repairs will end up being done by me, so I have pretty much stopped bringing up the issue.

By October most of the students clear out and we officially hit the slower time of the year here at the Stor'N'More. I don't mind of course, less business always means less heavy lifting and more watching television and waiting for the bell to ring as part of the plum assignment known as "office duty." Of course it also means that I will get less hours at work, since Dad doesn't like to pay me for watching TV. During the fall and winter months I'm pretty sure he starts regretting the idea of having to pay me at all.

In order to lure more customers this fall, I brought up the idea of a local ad campaign, highlighting the fact that our spaces are bigger than both the Storage Solutions down the street and the LockItAway on the other side of town. I even volunteered my acting services for such a venture. I would star as the clueless consumer straddled with an extra boat, motorcycle, and vintage Fender Stratocaster (all purchased for the commercial) while my father would narrate:

"...Don't want the wife to know about that boat? Worried about having to give up the Caddy in the divorce? Try Stor'N'More-We have the largest lockers in town-Your secrets are our secrets- forget the rest cause we are the best. Stor'N'More 1276 Highland Ave. Delecourte..."

Of course Dad always ignores my suggestions for marketing out of fear that he will have failed to comply with the rules and regulations found within the official franchise handbook binder, thus losing the right to have the Stor'N'More name and ugly blue and orange neon logo attached to our house. I don't really mind, after all fewer customers equal more free time for me. Instead of spending precious hours thinking about corrugated cardboard, and rental forms I could devote my energy to the important things in life like Cindy Crawford, Claudia Schiffer and Justine Weeks, goddess of Mr. Ralston's English class.

Chapter 2
Local Celebrity

To most Stor'N'More customers I am defined only by my nametag: I am just Steven, the kid who sells you a lock, hands you the contract and helps you load your belongings into the space you have rented. No one really notices me, they are too busy worrying about how secure our spaces are, or if their items will get damaged. I think this is just because of my age. People never really notice the kid who sells you your burger or delivers the pizza to your door. When my father is the one doing the selling people pay attention. They seem to really notice when he assures them that we have never had a break-in in our twenty year history, and we adhere to the Stor'N'More no water damage guarantee.

This doesn't bother me because I don't care whether or not people notice me at work, I only care if people know who I am at school, and I make sure they do. The popular kids may not know me by name but they always recognize that weird kid with too much gel in his dark brown hair, wearing some black Converse All Stars paired with fifties era clothing. Some people even say I bear a strange resemblance to my idol, missing rock'n'roll legend Ricky Stevenson.

Every once in a while my school and work life collide, usually with uncomfortable results. My friends and their families never seemed to be in need of a storage space, it's always one of the students who I don't really like or don't really know, who have been dragged here by one or both of their parents. Upon seeing me they are forced to acknowledge me and we always end up making rounds of forced small talk while Dad has their parent sign the endless array of official Stor'n'More--don't even try to sue us--forms. (By then I would be silently praying that this parent would not opt for the dreaded deluxe package.)

The small talk always consisted of whether or not there were bodies, or people living in our spaces and if I actually lived in the house separated from the office by a sliding door. Since the middle aged man schmoozing their parents into getting the deluxe package has the same dark brown hair and blue eyes as me, our shared lineage is pretty obvious. I can't pretend that I am just some kid with an after school job. I have to admit to this classmate that I barely know that yes, they have happened upon the house of Steve.

...

I was sitting back watching TV relishing the thought of having the rare day with no interruptions from the-ring-for-service-bell when I heard the sharp ding of the bell beckoning me to get back to work, I leapt from the couch. This wasn't because I was excited at the prospect of having a customer, but because I was hoping it would be something quick and easy so I could get back to the educational *Making of a Swimsuit Calendar* documentary I was watching.

Usually on slow autumn days a ring from the service bell means one of the customers wants to retrieve something from one of their spaces and has forgotten either their combination or how to open the gate entirely. It has been my experience that these customers are usually professors from the nearby university who have two or more PhD's.

Just as I walked through the door toward the counter my father came in through the office entrance and greeted the customer. I discreetly backed through the sliding door hoping that he hadn't noticed me, but as usual, my freedom turned out to be short lived. Within seconds I heard him yell out

"Steven, come out here and help us."

How convenient that Dad had forgotten I was supposed to be on office duty, helping people fill out the rental form, making them a replacement key, or selling them boxes, box cutters, masking tape and other storage paraphernalia. The tone of his voice informed me that this was not a request so I stepped outside and promptly found myself face to face with the one and only Linda Rand. Linda is the host of *Delacourte Delights!* Also known as that cheesy show after the news that highlights local town events and businesses. Of course this being Delacourte they once dedicated a whole show to The Crazy Castle: home of miniature golf, laser tag, and go karts.

It was my first on the job brush with a celebrity. Well, semi-celebrity. It's not like Elton John had stopped by and required help in loading carton after carton of pink boas, insane hats, and ridiculous sunglasses. Still it was something. Maybe her show would do a fascinating in depth look at what goes on inside all those local businesses that most people simply drive past. Or maybe she would notice my resemblance to Ricky Stevenson and would decide to create a whole show devoted to area teens who look like famous people.

Since I am the only one that would make the list, it would be an entire show devoted to me. I could see the admiring glances from my classmates already. Sure there would be hints of jealousy but it would mostly be awe especially from the popular kids. Even Linda's own super popular daughter Kelly never even had so much as a cameo role on her mother's show.

Mrs. Rand was wearing some sort of an overpriced pantsuit that looked like a reject from the Nancy Reagan catalog, her hair was shellacked and frosted, her lips were pursed in distaste, and she was glaring at me. I tried to shoot her a mega-watt smile but she didn't seem to notice so I nodded and followed her and Dad outside.

"I was on the radio once," I began, but Mrs. Rand ignored this and turned to my father.

"I need everything out that says Christmas, all the red and green bins, and everything in this corner. My Lord, we are running out of room," Mrs. Rand shifted from one high heel to the next before wandering back outside.

"Why is fifteen always rented out? Every time I have my husband inquire it is always taken. Surely there are not that many people in this town that need this much storage?"

"You'd be surprised," Dad said, but Linda wasn't paying attention. Instead she had wandered over to the soda machine parked in front of seventeen.

"Why is there a soda machine in front of this locker? How do the renters get in and out," She asked.

"That space is currently not available to rent," Dad said. "There are structural problems with the door."

"That certainly doesn't seem like a very solid business plan, does it?" Linda's eyes were still fixated on the soda machine. "You have a potential customer standing right in front of you and you can't rent out what is surely one of your largest most profitable units because of a door."

"Yes, I realize that and I can assure you it's a temporary situation. How about I put you on my special list and I will call you the second either fifteen or eighteen become available," Dad said. "We can set it up back in the office while Steven gets your boxes. Would you like a soda?"

As they started walking back to the office Linda yelled "Get out here and help these people," towards a rolled down window in her minivan. Jake Rand stepped out followed a second later by his sister Kelly.

Kelly followed me into the space and proceeded to start up a conversation. Though I am loathe to admit it now, there was once a time in my life when I would rush to tell all my friends I had just had an actual conversation with Kelly

Rand, cheerleader, homecoming princess, and spirit council chair. I would naively assume I was finally on my way to becoming popular and being invited to all the best parties. Fortunately I no longer had the insatiable need for a few seconds of popularity. I saw this for just what it was, just one of those moments where two people who have nothing in common are thrown together and temporarily bond out of sheer boredom.

The next time we saw each other we would no doubt return to barely acknowledging each other and staying true to our respective roles. Kelly as the head cheerleading queen of the school and me as that weird kid who shops at thrift stores and listens to oldies.

"Hey I know you," Kelly said as she picked out the smallest box she could find.

"You're in my English class." I responded.

"Oh yeah," she said. "So have you got your speech done yet?"

"Yeah I am almost done, I gotta give it on Tuesday," I told her, as we made our way towards the minivan.

"I have barely started mine, what with cheerleading and leadership, plus my mom making me with this stupid party. She never lets me help decorate, but she will make me unload boxes. At least you get paid for this," Kelly said as she set the box on one of the passenger seats of the van. Then she proceeded to wipe her hands on her jeans as if she had just handled a dead animal.

"I bet this party you guys have is really cool though. Wasn't it on TV last year?" I said, leaning against the hood of the minivan.

"It's on TV every year. That's the only reason why we even have it. So my Mom can impress people on her show. No one I know comes. Jake and I are not even allowed to have any people visit until it's over because she is so sure we will mess everything up. God it is so annoying." She rolled her eyes and glanced back over to the locker where Jake was lifting three crates that had *artificial pine* printed on them.

"I bet you guys get to have a real tree," she went on. "When I move out I'm always going to have real Christmas trees and I will use every single decoration my kids make on them."

She sighed as we walked back to the space where we grabbed a couple more small boxes to make it look as if we were working.

"So what exactly is in all of these crates?" I asked Kelly.

"Who knows?" she replied. "Every year my mom has a different theme for the party so she has to buy a lot of new stuff. Half the time it's not even that Christmassy you know, like last year it was this classical music theme. I had no idea that there were so many ornaments shaped like composers heads. My mom bought so much new stuff our basement got full so now we have to rent this space for all of it. We have to pull it out months early in order to have time to go through it, and decide on the new theme. I just know I am going to miss Jenny Hudson's sweet sixteen Saturday because I will be helping my mom inventory her ugly glass ornaments. I mean come on, it's not even Halloween yet."

I soon got the feeling she was getting tired of talking about the party and sure enough she changed the conversation by commenting on my clothes.

"I like your shirt."

"This one?" I had temporarily forgotten what I had put on this morning. I looked down and saw I was wearing an old bowling shirt with the name *Earl* embroidered on it that I had gotten for three dollars at Highland Thrift the other day.

"Yeah," Kelly went on. "Is that someone's actual bowling shirt? I mean, why would someone give it away?"

"Oh yeah I don't know," I said. "I was looking for a copy of *Sunset on Sunset* the other day when I saw it. I had to get it, 'cause genuine bowling shirts are totally hard to find."

"What's Sunset and Sunset?" she asked.

"*Sunset on Sunset*. It's an album by Ricky Stevenson and the Sleepers. The title song is about driving Sunset

Boulevard at Sundown. I am looking for an original vinyl copy not one of the reissues. I collect old records which is why I go to thrift stores occasionally, but *Sunset on Sunset* is damn near impossible to find," I explained.

"Cool," she replied. "My mom would kill me if I wore anything from a thrift store, maybe I should buy something just to piss her off." She glanced back towards our office where her mother was probably still issuing orders to my father then gave me a little smile. For a moment I wondered if I had just been instrumental in turning the future prom queen into a future rebel instead, but then I glanced at her Property of Delacourte High cheerleading squad T-shirt and thought, probably not.

...

After all of the stuff was loaded into the van I went back into our office. I assumed that Mrs. Rand would be either criticizing my father further or sulking in the corner but instead I found her smiling while Dad joked and tried to convince her that putting wrapping paper on our largest size boxes would make a good decoration for their screened in porch. Then he thanked her and shot her his million dollar smile.

Sooner or later middle aged women always melt in the presence of my father's smile. Even the most uptight ones like Linda Rand. It never fails.

Jack White is perhaps the most generic looking middle aged man on the face of the earth. He has your typical fifty-something male body; too much around the middle, and a chronically bad back that seems to flare up whenever he attempts any exercises to rectify the situation. As the years have progressed, his once thick black hair has definitely gotten grayer. My father has never been a person most people take any notice of, unless of course they are wondering how in the world he managed to end up married to Ellen White.

Everyone says Mom looks great for her age. She's thin and pretty, with chestnut brown hair she gets dyed regularly at a salon near the college. People always wonder what my mother could have possibly seen in my father, until he flashes his smile. Suddenly middle-aged women are like putty in his hands; even uptight types like Linda Rand can't resist it. I have spent hours trying to imitate that smile. Judging from the fact that I am usually sans pretty popular girlfriend (or any girlfriend at all), I must not have mastered it quite yet.

"God, what a pill that woman was. I hate dealing with people with a sense of entitlement" Dad said after the Rands had driven off. "I suppose it's because she's on that TV show. Thank goodness famous people don't often show up in this little town. Can you imagine having to deal with that all of the time?

"Then why were you kissing up to her," I asked. "Are you trying to score an invite to the shindig of the year?"

"We can't afford to lose her. Do you have any idea how hard it is to find renters for the extra large spaces?" Dad responded. "Obviously, Linda Rand is one of those women who simply loves to be catered to. Sometimes, if you give a person even a little of what they want you will find the reward is worth it. Besides she definitely has return customer written all over her, and this time of year we need all the return customers we can get."

"So you weren't trying to get invited to that party at all?" I asked. "You and Mom could get on TV.

"Trust me, if I had wanted to I could have gotten invited to parties a lot fancier than that, but they are absolutely not worth the effort. It's all people judging other people and worrying if you are wearing the right thing, driving the right car, or acting the right way. Trust me, Steven; it's even worse than high school. Once you have found your real friends always stick with them, they are all you really need."

I went away from our little father-son talk wondering just what the heck my delusional male parent had been talking about. Was Dad somehow convinced that somewhere out there lay a parallel universe where the owner of a small franchised storage facility was revered? If so then why wasn't he more prepared? The man doesn't even own a suit.

Chapter 3
Researching Ricky

For the first time in my entire life I had been given a homework assignment I wanted to do, and it was a speech of all things. My particular oral presentation was going to be on the life and mysterious disappearance of my idol: sixties rock'n'roll star Ricky Stevenson, who a lot of people claim I look just like. Dad had closed the Stor'N'More office for the night so I decided it was time to get back to work. I went up to my room and selected my visual aids. I decided to show two video clips chosen from my personal collection. The first one was a reenactment from an episode of *America Unexplained* and the other was an old interview with Ricky that they replayed on *Hollywood Truth's and Legends*.

I sorted through my footlocker full of video tapes until I found the two I wanted, then fast forwarded through each until I got to the spots I needed. When I finished, I set the tapes on my desk and walked over to my closet. This was particularly important because Justine Weeks is in my English class. With any luck, on the day of the speech, she would forget about whatever football player she was currently obsessing over, and instantly fall for me.

I decided to wear a red short sleeved shirt over a T-shirt and my 501's because Ricky wore a red shirt on the cover of his 1960 Album *Summertime Baby*. If I really do look like Ricky Stevenson, like some of my friends claim, I was going to milk it for all it's worth. After all, thousands of girls fell for Ricky back in the 1960's, all I wanted was one.

I went over to my closet to make sure the jeans and shirt were both reasonably clean when I heard the telltale steps of someone walking up our stairs. Since my parents (Dad especially--big surprise) always seemed to think I am way too obsessed with my look for the average teenage male, I was sure I couldn't convince either of them that flipping through my jeans constituted studying. I quickly walked over to my desk and began refreshing myself on the life story of Richard Martin Stevenson.

...

There are many critics who claim that disappearing off the face of the earth was the best public relations move Ricky Stevenson ever made. If it wasn't for his disappearance his band Ricky and the Sleepers, would have faded into obscurity, or become another group of fifty-something has beens that spent their summers playing the county fair and boardwalk circuit.

However, for every critic who claimed Ricky and the Sleepers were just another band playing bubblegum surf rock for teenage girls, there was another citing Ricky as a musical genius and comparing the band's third album *Sunset on Sunset* to the greats of that era like the Beach Boys' *Pet Sounds*.

Ricky and the Sleepers first attained popularity in 1959 when Ricky Stevenson was seventeen with the song *Not Another Teenage Breakup*. Both the song and its album, *Summertime Baby* went to number five on the charts. *Teenage Breakup* sounded pretty much like any other unremarkable bubblegum song of the era, with its two toned harmony and doo-wop flavor. If the Sleepers had continued in the same direction they would probably have been just another one hit wonder, but Ricky sensing that teenage love ballads were on the wane smartly switched over to California's burgeoning new surf rock scene after seeing a concert featuring a then relatively unknown young talent named Dick Dale.

Both critics and fans soon agreed that Ricky was one hell of a guitarist, and the Sleepers' fans appeared to be more than willing to follow the band into the new style. Their next album *Summer Ride* quickly rose to the top of the charts.

Despite an undeniable on-stage charisma, off stage Ricky was more famous for his moody behavior. The other members of the Sleepers; Carl Hansen, James, "Jamie" Underwood, and Robert "Bobby" Jenkins, basked in their popularity and became fixtures on the Los Angeles club circuit, but Ricky was rarely seen with them. He would usually shrug off his friends and instead choose to go for a solitary drive in his turquoise blue and white '59 Corvette. These drives often ended up lasting for days.

Ricky's mood swings and disappearing acts vanished however, when Carl introduced him to Elaine Peterson, a young UCLA co-ed. It appeared to be love at first sight and the other band members were sure that eventually the two would marry. When Elaine was around Ricky returned to his charismatic on stage persona and the Sleepers recorded their most successful album *Sunset on Sunset*.

Unfortunately Ricky's happiness was short lived. The following year while the Sleepers went on a nationwide tour promoting their album *The Palmdale Sessions*, Elaine who had stayed behind to finish her classes, was killed in car accident on her way home from a party. Her date had been Ken Mitchell, a popular UCLA football player who walked away from the accident with barely a scratch. He was arrested for driving while intoxicated, but the charges were eventually dropped.

Rumors abounded that Ricky and Elaine had been in a huge fight before he left for the tour and he blamed himself for her death. Several of Elaine's college friends later stated that she had grown tired of the mobs of teenagers who accosted Ricky wherever he went. Unbeknownst to Ricky, who was on tour, Elaine and Ken were getting very serious, and were making plans to marry after graduation.

Elaine's death became a turning point in Ricky's life and career. He somehow got through the rest of the tour but once he returned home, Ricky quickly went back to his old ways of vanishing for days and even weeks at a time.

The Sleepers' label Emcee records had done their best to hide the truth, until one day in December 1963 when Ricky spent the night in jail after passing out in front of a bar in Barstow, California. Gossip circulated that the Sleepers' next album *Drive into the Sky* was going to be a disaster because Ricky hardly ever showed up, and when he was there, he didn't put his heart into any of the songs.

When *Drive into the Sky* came out in April of 1964, the rumors of a disappointing effort by Ricky Stevenson were proven untrue. Instead, many critics hailed it as one of his best efforts. Recording the album had seemed to be cathartic for Ricky. *Drive into the Sky* had packed more of an emotional punch than some of his previous records, yet was still hailed as a crowd pleaser.

Ricky himself seemed better as well. The Sleepers did two Los Angeles area shows to promote the album and at each one, Ricky gave a stellar performance, even staying afterward to greet some of his fans and mingle at some Hollywood parties.

Happy with the successful results of the two shows, Ricky's bandmates and his label began pressuring Ricky to once again embark on a summer tour. He finally relented and the tour was scheduled to begin on June 9th.

On the morning of June 1st, 1964 both Jamie Underwood, drummer for the Sleepers and Robert Stevenson, Ricky's father found mysterious notes from Ricky attached to their doors. Jamie and the other band members believed it was a suicide note, because Ricky had made a reference to the Ricky and the Sleepers' song *Another Mississippi Morning,* about a man who kills himself by driving into a river. The permanence of Ricky's decision was further cemented once they arrived and found the front door slightly ajar. Inside the place had been cleaned out, and Ricky himself was nowhere to be found.

Within a matter of days rumors were flying that Ricky Stevenson was gone for good. Soon after, the press had gotten wind of the story and Ricky's disappearance became front page news when Jamie gave a copy of his note to a reporter at the *Los Angeles Times*. (The contents of the note given to Robert Stevenson were never disclosed to the public.) Reports of a young man spotted in a blue and white Corvette started coming in from all over the country, but each one proved to be a dead end. Still most of America seemed convinced that Ricky was not dead, but had disappeared on purpose. This theory was further fueled by revelations that his bank accounts had been cleared out, and by a tabloid magazine who had published several photos of Ricky's empty house.

In an effort to locate its biggest moneymaker, Emcee records quickly teamed up with radio stations all across America, holding several contests that offered prizes and substantial cash rewards to anyone who could locate Ricky.

Those who had known Ricky personally believed he had been suicidal.

"He was never quite the same after Elaine's death," said bandmate Carl Hansen. "Every time Ricky was out in public it was just an act, he was uncomfortable at premieres and parties, and he couldn't stand being mobbed every time he tried to cross the street."

Friends also cited his troubled relationship with his father, Robert, an apartment manager in Van Nuys, California.

"Ricky and Bob never got along that well. His mother had died when he was really young, and Ricky never felt that his father was there for him. I think that's why he cleared out his money and his stuff. He knew his father would end up with the royalties from his estate and he didn't want him to get the money in the bank accounts as well. Ricky probably buried it somewhere--or maybe he really did drive into the river with most of his belongings and cash at his side. That wouldn't surprise me at all," said Ricky's longtime friend Ralph Kendall.

Whether Ricky lived or died, he ceased being just another rock and roll star and became a legend that June day. As with most legends, the more time passed, the more famous Ricky Stevenson became. When the months wore into years it became more and more clear that Ricky was probably dead, since no sightings of him ever proved to be accurate. Every year on the anniversary of the disappearance, radio stations would play marathons of Ricky's music, fans would hold candlelight vigils, and hundreds would flock to Ricky's Pacific Palisades estate.

There were numerous crackpots declaring themselves Ricky or claiming they had real proof about what had happened to him. In 1980 an entertainment television show caused a huge controversy when they found a Richard Stevenson in Amarillo, Texas who asserted he was Ricky. It later turned out he was just trying to get business into his failing carpet store. Several copycats followed, including a pharmacist, a veterinarian, and even a Ricky Stevenson tribute artist from Las Vegas, Nevada.

Throughout the summer of 1964 there were tips from several people who claimed that they had seen a blue and white Corvette drive recklessly near the Mississippi River, just outside of St. Louis, Missouri. Two months later the River was dredged in several places but no trace of Ricky or his car was found.

In 1985 an elderly man, John P. Winfield, claimed that a young man had come to him during the summer of 1964 and had offered to pay him $6,000 to store a Corvette in his St. Paul, Minnesota garage until 1982 when he planned to return for it. Since 1982 had come and gone with the young men never returning, Winfield made the decision to put the car up for auction three years later. The media went into a frenzy when it was discovered that the car's old California plates read CLJ 412 a match of Ricky's.

Sensing a good publicity move, a prestigious New York auction house offered to handle the auction for less than their usual rate, and Mr. Winfield agreed. Unfortunately, he didn't realize that the auction house had a professional team of appraisers standing by. On the eve of the auction the car was deemed a fake since the VIN numbers did not match those of the Corvette bought by Ricky. It was later revealed that Winfield was a known con artist who had spent time in prison.

The auction was immediately canceled and Winfield was arrested and later sentenced to probation, while the car was seized by the federal government. Winfield's contact that had made up the phony license plate was never caught. The car was later resold at a Government seizure auction and fetched upwards of 50,000 dollars. In 1989 the scandal surrounding the car was made into a highly rated TV Movie titled *The Greatest Hoax in Rock and Roll History*.

Chapter 4
How I Became Ricky's Biggest Fan

My speech went great and not only was I sure that I got an A, but Justine was listening, I could sense it. Not once in the many times I glanced over at her direction did she look the slightest bit bored unlike with Dan "the Man" Parker's long, boring tirade on Michael Jordan. She had to be sleeping through that one for sure. With any luck, my speech would help Justine become a fan of Ricky Stevenson and consequently of me, after all it always seemed that the girls who liked me had a thing for vintage rock and roll. In fact it was through the attention of a girl that I had become a fan of Ricky in the first place.

It was just before Halloween in eighth grade and I was sitting in English class working on a group project. Our group wasn't getting much work done, as usual. Group reports were usually just an excuse for teachers to put four people together who had nothing in common, in order to see how they would interact. Would we manage to put together a report where all the parts corresponded with each other in equal amounts? From my experiences these presentations usually ended up being a jumbled assortment of four different ramblings loosely tied together only by the subject. Often the bulk of the project would be accomplished by one overachiever while three slackers stood around holding badly done visual aids scrawled on poster board.

Aside from me, our group consisted of Mike Stewart, who would be of no help to the project unless the subject was boogers, fart jokes, or pyromania, Jill Jensen who I didn't really know that well, and her best friend, Wendy Summers. Despite the fact that she was born the year he died, Wendy had the unusual distinction of being Taft Jr. High's only Elvis Presley fan.

"Elvis? You like Elvis? Dude, I thought only my mom liked him. How come you like some 300 pound guy who died on the toilet while choking on a ham sandwich?" Mike asked Wendy after she pulled out a folder with a *Jailhouse Rock* era photo of the king emblazoned upon its cover.

"He didn't die eating a ham sandwich that was some chick from the Mamas and the Papas," she said. "Anyway back in the fifties he was really cute. Besides I don't just like Elvis I like a lot of different musicians. Look I have a Ricky Stevenson notebook too. See--not Elvis."

Wendy sighed and set the Ricky notebook on her desk then she looked up in my direction.

"Oh my God, you look exactly like him. I can't believe I never noticed before," Wendy said.

Jill quickly concurred while Mike just snorted. Though I had never particularly cared what Mike Stewart thought, I was at the age where the opinions of females were beginning to matter more than ever.

I looked down at the notebook, Ricky Stevenson just seemed to be your average greaser to me but both girls were looking at me in a way no girl had ever before. Up until that day I had spent my whole life unsuccessfully trying to be a jock, despite my accident prone nature which always tended to flare up in inopportune moments during gym class. I never liked sports that well because I was probably the most uncoordinated boy in my elementary school. Back in the first grade I gained the dubious distinction of being the first student to ever get a concussion from an overinflated dodgeball. What was really sad was I wasn't even playing dodgeball when it happened, I had been walking towards the drinking fountain when Matt Kingsley's throw managed to pass over the students in the middle of the circle where it bounced off another student on the perimeter and landed squarely between my eyes squashing my nose, and knocking me to the ground.

I never had much use for the game of dodgeball after that. I also had a dislike of kickball, resulting from the time I tripped over my shoelaces on my way to first base, and I was never a big fan of steal the bacon, because I don't recall ever once managing to get the eraser safely back to my side without getting tagged. Physical activity was something I only pretended to enjoy. Like every other male to ever walk the halls of Taft Jr. High, I had been led to believe that a talent in sports was the only way to win the heart of your average adolescent female, at least until you were old enough for car ownership. Wendy however, with her finger pointing towards the notebook cover, seemed to be offering a magical alternative.

Later that day I took my bike and headed over to Wahl's drugs and bought myself a pocket version of the notebook, then I proceeded down the street to Highland Thrift. Highland was a store I had lived down the street from my whole life, but had never before dared to venture into. As I walked toward the door my eyes swept from side to side. I honestly didn't know what I was so afraid of. It's not like any of my classmates lived anywhere near Highland.

I lingered for a few minutes outside the store, staring at its stark white painted brick exterior and reading the faded paint on the plate glass windows. When I finally grew tired of peering at lettering reading *Lowest Prices in Town!*, and *Super Senior discounts every Tuesday!*, I took a deep breath, took one last look up and down Highland to make sure no one under the age of thirty five was coming this way, and stepped inside.

Who cares if someone sees me, I told myself. After all I am just here to purchase a Halloween costume for the dance. Everyone knew that last year Jake Rand wore an old cheerleading outfit he got at the Salvation Army over on Chestnut, and his portrayal of blood soaked demonic cheerleader Tiffany Cambridge from *Suburban Pom Pom Massacre 3* won him the dance's costume contest.

Once inside, I took a deep breath and absorbed the musty smell that seemed to permeate everything. Until that day I had thought that mustiness was an odor I had gotten acclimated to because of the hundreds of boxes had been moved from basements into our storage spaces over the years.

The front portion of Highland Thrift was taken up by furniture covered in the ugliest colors and patterns I had ever seen, the clothing took up most of the middle and the rest of the stuff was towards the back and along the walls of the store. Two college students stood in the furniture portion debating whether or not to buy a heavy carved wooden coffee table that had been stained a most unfortunate shade of avocado green.

The only other customer was an older woman who was, from the looks of it, having an animated conversation with herself. I did my best to avoid any sort of eye contact with her by looking down at the store's mustard colored shag carpet as I made my way towards the racks of men's shirts. Much to my amazement I found a blue short sleeved shirt that looked like it would work. Since I was not about to go into some scary thrift store changing room, I slipped it over my T-shirt. It was a perfect fit.

The price of the shirt was also right. A buck fifty for a perfectly good shirt? I stood for a couple of seconds amazed at such a deal. The rest of the outfit I had in my closet at home so I wandered over to the sunglasses section, which was actually a bin full of old sunglasses perched on a stained

1950's era dresser missing three of its drawers. Unfortunately the bin didn't seem to have anything good, it was just a pile of those horrendously large sunglasses women wore in the late 1970s.

As I turned away from the dresser, the door chimes jangled. Out of instinct I glanced up, only to find my eyes locking with those of Rob McIntyre, older brother of my friend Dave.

"Hey Stevie, what's up" he said (only the older and larger can get by with calling me Stevie--if anyone else tries it they are dead.)

I hesitated a second while the thoughts raced through my head. Surely by tomorrow everyone at both Taft Junior High and Delacourte High School would have heard how young Steven White had been spotted shopping with the crazies at Highland Thrift. Rumors would surly fly that my family was sinking into poverty. We would quickly lose most of our customers out of the fear that we would need to hold a huge storage auction and rummage sale consisting of their belongings in order to survive.

Fortunately, a few seconds later rational thought took over and I was able to calm myself down. Rob was also here of his own free will wasn't he and besides I was simply here to find an unusual Halloween costume.

"Oh umm, Hey Rob what's up? I am just trying to find stuff for my Halloween outfit-cause my school's having this dance in a couple of days," I replied, wondering exactly what he was doing here anyway.

"Oh yeah, the eighth grade Halloween dance, I remember that," Rob said. "None of the girls in my class even danced, they just sat on the bleachers and compared their costumes, and the music, dude, they played the worst music, but then again, it was eighth grade. I had the absolute worst taste in music back then. I was into white boy rap and stuff. I mean, what was I thinking?"

"Oh yeah," I mumbled not sure what to say--did this mean he thought I listened to white boy rap--dear god I hoped not.

The older brothers of my friends always seemed to fall into two separate categories. There were the ones who wanted to beat us up, and then there were those whom we someday wanted to become. Rob had always fallen into the second category. His room was a wonderland of blacklite posters featuring classic rock icons like Hendrix, the Grateful Dead and The Who. Whenever he was home Rob always seemed to be in his garage practicing guitar with his band UltraViolet. Sometimes when we were bored (which was all too often sad to say) Dave, I, and whoever else was around would sit on the hood of Rob's Gremlin and watch an impromptu concert taking place in his garage.

UltraViolet never got anywhere near good because every time they played they were eventually forced to stop by either Dave's mom or his perpetually cranky neighbor, Mr. Knoll. I could never figure out why Mr. Knoll bothered. The members of UltraViolet would only heed his pleas for an hour or so, resuming once they realized that they needed more practice if they were going to win the upcoming battle of the bands. It was always a battle of the bands; if UltraViolet ever played any other gig I sure don't remember it.

"Hey Steve, I'm going over to check out the tunes if you wanna come," Rob said.

Together we walked towards the back wall where there were several crates of old records. Rob must have been either really bored or in a charitable mood, because for some reason he kept on talking to me as we browsed.

"So, I came here because last week my friend Jeff scored this really sweet reel to reel for only twenty bucks." (I didn't have the guts to tell Rob that I had no idea what the heck a reel to reel was) "But of course they have absolutely nothing whenever I swing by," he said. "The trouble with this town is all the college students and the used record store owners get to all the good stuff before I do. I bet all the thrift stores out in the boonies like Hainesville have got tons of the good stuff because you know all they listen to out there is like country and shit. I totally have to get the Gremster running so I can take a little roadtrip out there you know."

Rob glanced up at me for a second and started talking again. "Hey Stevie, do me a favor will you? If you see anything good, like Floyd or Hendrix, you have to grab it for me okay?"

"Sure," I said, "but I am not seeing much."

Not seeing much was an understatement. In front of me seemed to be a sea of *Herb Alpert and the Tijuana Brass*, mixed with old church choir Christmas albums, and occasionally broken up by *The Carpenters, John Denver,* or a *Barbara Streisand* album. It was pretty much like someone had cloned my grandparent's record collection several times and transplanted it here.

Since I was pretty sure the musical stylings of Herb Alpert wouldn't make Rob's cool list, I found myself starting a new conversation.

"So what do you think of Ricky Stevenson?" I asked.

"Hmmm, Ricky Stevenson," he replied. "The late fifties early sixties isn't really my era you know, but compared to a lot of the singers back them Ricky had chops. He was definitely one of the best guitarists of that era and it's cool how he mysteriously vanished. When I get famous I am totally going to do that but only for a year or so not for like twenty or whatever. I think he must be dead because why would you disappear for that long when you could have some seriously hot chicks surrounding you at concerts?"

"Oh yeah totally--that would be sweet," I said.

"Why do you ask?" Rob continued. "Have they got some Ricky Stevenson over there? Some of his records are worth tons."

"Oh, uh no," I said "they don't have any of his records-that I can see, it's just I was going to go as him for

Halloween, cause some people say I kinda look like him I guess."

Rob squinted at me and said "Yeah I can sorta see a little resemblance you could probably pull that off, with some vintage fifties clothes and a guitar."

"Yeah I was hoping maybe they would have a guitar here, 'cause I don't really have much money right now, but I didn't see any," I said.

"A guitar in a thrift store, you have got to be trippin man. No one would *ever* donate a guitar to a thrift store. Hell most of the time the used ones are worth more than the new ones. Trust me man, thrift stores don't ever have guitars, but hey, if you need a coffee maker," he said pointing to a set of shelves that contained about a hundred used coffeemakers. "If I were you I would check out the classifieds and Richardson's Music, maybe they're having a sale."

A few minutes later Rob and I parted. He left empty handed while I went over and purchased my new shirt. Not only had I survived my very first thrift store encounter but I had a distinct feeling I would return.

That ending up being pretty much the longest conversation I ever had with Rob McIntyre. He's still around attending Dexter Community College, and I occasionally still see him browsing the racks at Highland Thrift. (He has a working car now but I guess the Hainesville thrift store doesn't cater to his needs.) UltraViolet broke up after he graduated but I recently heard a rumor that he is trying to start a new band with his college buddies tentatively called InfraRed. Needless to say, my friends and I have no plans to catch their next act.

Chapter 5
My Epic 8th Grade Halloween Flashback

When you spend your whole childhood getting free candy on a certain fall night, it comes as a rude shock to ones system to be asked: "Aren't you a little old to be trick or treating?" If my friends and I had our way we would be trick or treating until we were a least 40, but alas the rest of our little city doesn't quite see it this way.

Our bodies are programmed to go crazy every Oct. 31st, in anticipation of a rush of glorious chocolate splendor. Every year hundreds of local eighth graders would eat almost all of the candy meant to be passed out to local kindergartners by their families, and many would ransack the candy filled pillowcases of younger siblings not unlike a bloodthirsty pirate. In order to quell this wave of chocolate fueled mania a few years ago the powers that be within the Chalmers County School Board devised a cunning plan and thus the annual William Howard Taft Junior High School Halloween Dance was born.

I hadn't managed to convince my mother to purchase an electric guitar for my costume but she did purchase me a pair of black Converse All Stars for the occasion. (I think that the fact that you could actually see most of my big toe peeking through the toe of one of my old sneakers helped to convince her they were a necessity.) I wore the all-stars with my 501's rolled at the cuff and a white T-shirt with the blue thrift shirt over it. To get fifties greaser hair I put half the bottle of gel into my thick dark brown mane. My hair didn't move but at least it looked pretty authentic. I next put on the sunglasses that I had spent most of my allowance on and I stuck a comb in my back pocket for the final detail.

"Steven you look very cute. Doesn't he Jack?" my mother said as I stood in the kitchen showing off my costume before the dance.

"Whatever you do don't go near an open flame with all that stuff on your hair," was his reply.

Mom and I ignored Dad's comment and proceeded outside where we climbed into our station wagon, and headed off towards the dance.

The dance started out the way most junior high dances do, a mixture of crappy, lame and boring as hell, especially for those of us lacking a girlfriend--a camp my friends and I seemed to be perpetually stuck in. My crowd went to get away from their families, and to see if there was any decent food. As usual, my friends and I ended up by the food tables disappointed in the lack of anything good.

"Du-ude I am so going to steal all of my little brothers candy," Chris Jenkins said as he reached towards a bowl of store brand chocolate creme cookies. Our school was apparently so cheap it bought the imitation ones with almost no filling. I guess purchasing genuine Oreos would instantly send the budget into a downward spiral and cause a county-wide teacher's strike. I looked up from the refreshment table and noticed that the dance didn't seem that crowded. Maybe my smarter classmates had decided to go trick or treating one last time.

Even worse, none of my friends seemed to get my costume.

"Dude did you even dress up?" Joey Hertz asked me.

"Yes I dressed up. I am Ricky Stevenson-duh," I responded, and thrust my pocket version of the notebook at him.

"Oh well you should have brought a guitar because it looks like you're just this guy in a T-shirt and jeans," he said cooly.

So of course I rolled my eyes at him (Why was I even friends with these people anyway?) and responded

"Do you know how much a guitar costs? What am I supposed to do? Buy one with my allowance from this week?"

"Maybe you should have gotten a shirt with Ricky's picture on it so people would know that's who you are supposed to be," suggested Stuart Meeley.

God! Even Stuart Meeley with his always running nose and croaky voice was dissing my costume!

"Ricky Stevenson would never wear a shirt with his own picture on it. You guys just don't know anything about music" I grumbled then turned my head and looked towards the dance floor.

It is almost a universally known fact that dances where the girls stand on one end of the room while the boys stand at the other is a myth made up by the people who write episodes of cornball TV shows. Our dance featured plenty of people dancing, but they fell into two groups; the permanent inseparable couples who were into slow songs, and the popular crowd, who danced in clumps of five to ten people and preferred the faster songs so they could sing along at the key points. When a fast song was going on you would here a cheer of "Jump!" or "Yeah Baby" every five minutes or so.

"Maybe we should go down and dance; I've been practicing my moves." Stuart suggested as we watched a crowd of popular kids doing some sort of a dance with either an Egyptian or a chicken related theme.

"Uhh--Stuart we are all guys over here--I dunno about you but I would rather dance with some girls," Joey said, thus getting a laugh from the rest of our pathetic little clique.

Stuart remained undaunted, however.

"Du-ude, once we start dancing the girls will come. I mean just look at how many are on the bleachers just waiting for some guys to start dancing so they can join in.

The rest of my friends looked down at their feet and grumbled sayings like:

"Well feel free Stuart, it's all you," or "My feet sorta hurt you guys go on ahead." Predictably we all stayed put.

I glanced up toward where Stuart had been talking about. There were an awful lot of girls sitting on the bleachers, but they didn't exactly look like they were on the edge of their seats waiting for one of us to ask them to dance. Instead they were sitting in clumps talking with their friends and getting up often in smaller groups to check their hair and makeup in the girls bathroom. My eyes locked with Wendy Summers and much to my amazement she started dragging a group of her friends my way.

Unlike my somewhat dense friends, Wendy got my costume right away.

"Oh my God! You went as Ricky Stevenson, I was totally right you look just like him! Don't you guys agree?" she asked her friends.

"Oh yeah totally, uhh huh," they nodded and murmured simultaneously.

For a few precious moments my normal friends had seemed to vanish. Who cared about Chris, Stuart, Dave, Joey or any of them when I was in the presence of *women*. Then the next thing I knew Wendy had somehow convinced everybody to head for the dance floor. Instead of just the popular kids it was Wendy and I and the rest of our friends who were bouncing around yelling "Jump Baby Jump!" or "Come On Come On!" while we watched Stuart show us his "moves" which were a mishmash of portions of outdated dances like the Roger Rabbit and the Moonwalk.

Looking back on it now you would think this memory would embarrass me. We were all so gawky back in junior high. Though I don't exactly know what was I thinking dancing to songs with the words "Come On Come On!" in them, somehow the eighth grade Halloween dance ended up becoming a turning point in my humble little life. I didn't win the costume contest that night, but I didn't care-because I had gained the attention of people who would help my all important social status in two ways. In the first place, they were ever so slightly more popular than me and more importantly, they were members of that elusive and mysterious opposite sex. Plus I had also had way more fun than anyone would ever expect to get out of your typical adolescent mating ritual.

For all these reasons, I never wanted to take my costume off. Of course I did that night, but from that moment on I knew I would do whatever it took to make any girl I met realize I look just like someone famous (and hopefully in their opinion--cute) regardless of the opinions of my loser friends. Even more amazingly, most of my crowd stopped razzing me continually after that dance. Evidently Dave, Stuart, Joey, and the rest of my friends had discovered that being near someone girls wanted to hang out with had actually become a good thing.

I started to pomade my hair up every day and buying more and more 50's style clothes, until I pretty much looked like Ricky every day. Halloween became a tradition of all out Ricky-ness. So much so that I shocked everyone last year by going as Elvis.

Chapter 6
Rock and Roll Runaway

My new commitment of looking like Ricky Stevenson, naturally made me want to know more about him. I didn't know anything at first, but cable TV is full of documentaries on him. There is also the 1977 movie about his life *Rock and Roll Runaway* starring Ken Stafford, which I promptly bought a used copy of at University Video. One of my ultimate fantasies is that someday Hollywood will decide to remake this movie, realize they need someone unknown, come to the Midwest for casting and of course, discover me.

I know I could do a way better job of playing Ricky than Ken Stafford did. Sure he did get nominated for an Oscar, but Ken Stafford looks nothing like Ricky Stevenson. Especially in the scene where the Sleepers were about to get discovered while playing at a bar mitzvah. Instead of concentrating on what is one of the most pivotal scenes in the whole movie, I kept waiting for Ken's ugly black wig to fall off his normally blond head. I also wanted Carl Kramer who played Ben's uncle Dave, the Emcee records talent scout, to stop spouting hackneyed lines like.

"He's good as gold. Pure gold. That kid has got it!"

I discovered Ricky Stevenson's music when I purchased a CD of *Ricky! A Retrospective*, the greatest hits collection

Emcee records had rushed out after his disappearance. I didn't think I would like it, but of course I did. How can you not like a guy who plays a guitar that well? Ricky can take sole credit for me switching my taste in music from the crap they played on *Pop 92 (your dance station!)* to the fifties and sixties music they play on *Rockin Oldies 101*.

The summer after eighth grade when I finally started getting paid for working for my father, I saved up enough for my own guitar, Lu Lu Belle. Soon most of my paychecks were going towards lessons with Mr. Mackie who works at Richardson's music downtown. Mr. Mackie told me I have an innate talent, though when I hear myself play I have no idea what he is talking about. I assumed that this was just a line he gave all his students so they would keep coming back to him in order to really develop that "innate talent." I think you can guess by now that my goal is to play just like Ricky Stevenson. I can do some of his surf riffs well, but I know I am nowhere near his level, which is why I continue to take lessons even now.

I often told myself that I am not as good as Ricky because I don't have enough time to practice with Dad working me constantly, but I know that can't be the reason. After several viewings of *Rock and Roll Runaway*, I know that Ricky spent most of his time repairing various apartments in his father's building or cleaning out the filter to the complex's pool. He only made time to practice when he was especially mad at his father, Bob. One of the most famous scenes is the one where Ricky had a huge fight with his dad about taking over managerial duties at the apartment building after graduation. After the fight was over he climbed up on the building's rooftop and played all night long, ignoring the shouts from the tenants down below. That scene was later parodied by a sketch comedy show when it ran a sketch featuring a yodeler having a fight with his father about taking over the family bratwurst business, then going up to an apartment rooftop and yodeling all night long.

Even though I think the all night guitar scene may have been an exaggeration, I do believe most of the plot of *Rock and Roll Runaway*. Thanks to a replay on *The Vintage Network* I also have a tape of Ricky doing his most famous televised interview on *Ted Ferris Tonight*. I discovered that if you watch the interview then the movie, you will realize that ninety percent of *Rock and Roll Runaway's* plot was lifted directly from Ricky's January, 1964 sit down with Ted Ferris.

It's all there. When Ricky was not reminiscing about good times spent at the local burger joint, he was expounding on his decision to teach himself guitar to infuriate his father, and describing the humble origins of Ricky and the Sleepers. Ricky had started the band in order to make extra cash playing parties and dances around the San Fernando Valley, but it was his chance meeting with Jamie Underwood at a local bowling tournament that would eventually lead the Sleepers to stardom. After the Sleepers original drummer, Roy Kingman quit in order to attend Stanford, Jamie agreed to join the band under one condition: they would have to play the bar mitzvah of the son of Jamie's father's employer, Max Horowitz. Ricky and the other members agreed and the rest was history. Perhaps it was somewhat ironic that none of the members of the band were Jewish, but in the words of the late Dave Horowitz:

"Talent is talent plus that boy Ricky has definitely got the look that all the girls want."

Many of *Rock and Roll Runaway's* facts have been further corroborated in several of the books written about Ricky Stevenson's life. The book many believe to be the most accurate portrayal of Ricky's life was *Ricky Ricky: Where Have You Gone?* by his high school friend Terry Albertson. I have a copy sitting on the shelf over my desk but sadly it's not the much sought after first edition. Anyway I tend to believe *Ricky Ricky: Where Have You Gone?* a lot more than my cheap paperback copy of last year's *Ricky the Unauthorized Story!*, which claims Ricky ran away because he refused to become an FBI informant against the mob.

...

After my experience with the costume, I discovered that Highland and the other area thrift stores were the best place to get the vintage look as cheaply as possible. This was something that my friends were not as quick to embrace however. For the most part they wanted to hang out at the mall and they all regarded my new shopping habits as an unfortunate quirk that would hopefully go away soon. I was sick of trying to explain myself to them; it seemed to me that I had two choices: one, I could continue to try to get the girl by trying to look like Ricky Stevenson-teen idol, or two: I could try to get the girl by having my mother buy me ill-fitting ugly flannel shirts in bulk from J.C. Penney's like Stuart Meeley's mother did.

Quite naturally I decided to stick with option number one, because it sort of worked. Wendy Summers and her crowd started hanging out with us lot more once we hit high school. None of us were involved in a hot and heavy romance, but it was very convenient to have a group of females handy for taking to homecoming dances and various other school activities.

I had a superstition that my uncanny resemblance to Ricky Stevenson was somehow lucky. Deep down I had this feeling that if I were to give up my Ricky look and try to look like everyone else, I would more or less instantly return to my loser pre-eighth grade Halloween dance status. This fear drove me on a perpetual quest to try and channel Ricky's essence even more, including my unsuccessful recent attempts to get my friends to start a Sleepers-esque band. It was a lost cause and I knew it. None of my friends were into oldies like I was, and the only one of them who played an instrument was Stuart. Unfortunately the average surf rock tribute band has little use for a trombonist, no matter how competent he may be.

Since high school is not a time when you can just drop the friends you have and expect to make new ones, I simply put up with the ones I had. I often found myself hanging out with them at the mall bored out of my mind in front of the pretzel shack while they debated buying expensive shirts with the logo of whatever sports brand was big that week. I never understood why my mostly scrawny friends thought that wearing a shirt that said *Nike* on it would instantly make them into a jock.

I usually ended up buying nothing at the mall, instead opting to do my personal shopping alone. This mostly consisted of going to Highland or one of the other local thrift emporiums and checking out records first then the clothing racks while avoiding eye contact with the usual weirdos and wishing that Rob McIntyre had been closer to my age.

As my life continued down this pattern, I wondered if I was crazy for wanting to save some money by shopping cheaply. I saw college students in thrift stores all the time just never anyone my own age. Often at the mall I would look to see if there were any new clothes I wanted--but the styles were never right, and they always seemed to cost a ton. I also noticed that I seemed to have more of my own money than most of my friends who were always begging their parents for enough cash to see a movie or get a bite to eat. Even my friends who had after school jobs were always blowing their paychecks on thirty dollar T-shirts or hundred dollar sneakers, yet I could never get them to change their ways. I had given up hope on ever meeting someone I could relate to until the day the new kid came to town.

Chapter 7
The New Kid in Town

By the beginning of junior year I had almost given up on finding anyone with my particular taste in stores, music, or anything else. Then I met the new kid in town. Greg Lewis had just moved to Delacourte and he and his dad stopped by in order to unload their space. Mr. Lewis had the deluxe package which includes the use of a deluxe Stor'N'More handcart as well as loading and unloading assistance by a courteous and caring Stor'N'More employee. I am usually that employee. It's funny how every time a deluxe package is purchased either Dad just "remembered" some office paperwork he needs to catch up on, or his back has conveniently started giving him spasms.

I liked both Greg and his father Dan immediately, probably because they were the type of people who realized that the assistance that comes with the deluxe package is in fact *assistance*--not sit on your lazy behind and stare at me while I move box after box of your heavy worthless crap into a poorly lit storage space. Both Greg and his father actually helped. Lucky for me, they were some of the most talkative people ever to step within the city limits of Delacourte. Loading up storage lockers goes a lot faster if you are actively involved in a conversation.

The second I met Greg he noticed my shirt.

"Cool shirt--is that vintage?" he asked.

"Yeah," I responded.

'Yeah, My Grandma owns the Antique Attic and my whole family is into antiques. Vintage clothes can be worth something and I usually get dibs on the coolest stuff" Greg said.

"Cool," I said noticing for the first time he was wearing a similar shirt.

We then went to work loading up the space. Amongst the many boxes I spotted a fifties era coffee table, a tall stone tiki statue, and a large stuffed fish that looked like it came from a restaurant. As we worked, Greg told me his life story.

"Yeah Grandma owns the building her store is in and the restaurant inside went under so we are taking over the space. We are hoping the college will bring in a crowd that is more into good food than Monroeville. My Dad is a great chef, but he hates just making fried chicken and hamburgers all the time, plus there is a great space for a bar inside, not so much a rowdy college bar, but something more sophisticated you know. Maybe if our restaurant is successful we can make it into a chain," Greg exahaled as he grabbed a large carton but then he started back up a second later.

"Dad has always wanted to own a restaurant in a city but the rents are like super high. We figure we should get the formula right somewhere small first, then expand. Do you think a Polynesian theme is too dated? We are thinking of trying for a resurgence, but with a little more sophistication, while still keeping the tongue in cheek attitude..."

Woah, didn't this guy ever give you a chance to get a word in edgewise? I wondered. Oh well who cares--he liked my shirt.

"So did you get that shirt at an antique store or what?" he asked.

"No umm there's this thrift store down the street. I ummm collect records and sometimes I see other stuff I like, you know," I responded.

I am always hesitant when talking about this subject because you never know how people will react when they hear the dreaded combination of the words thrift and store.

"Oh yeah--cool, my dad and I are always headed to local thrift shops to find stuff we can sell at Grandma's place, plus you may have noticed my dad is into vintage decor. We are always at estate sales, garage sales, and thrift stores looking for a deal. You have got to show me some of the shops you know," he said.

When Greg started classes, he ended in up my homeroom. Since I was the only person his age he had met prior to starting school, Greg ended up sitting with me and my friends in our corner of the cafeteria. I was pretty sure this wouldn't last too long however, since Greg seemed to be one of those magical people who made friends within two seconds of meeting someone. As we walked the halls suddenly echoes of "hey what's up," seemed to be directed towards our crowd at a much higher rate than usual. I knew this couldn't possibly last, and was sure that by the end of the week Greg would be joking around with Matt Kingsley and Jake Rand, running for class president, and dating Kelly Rand or even--God forbid--Justine Weeks. At least that's what I thought until lunchtime, when Greg sat down on some benches and he kicked up his feet, revealing a pair of bowling shoes in blue and red with the number ten clearly printed on the back.

"Umm why are you wearing bowling shoes?" Dave asked.

"Aren't they cool?" Greg said with a goofy smile. "No I know what you are thinking I didn't steal them. My best friend back in Monroeville; Jeff, gave me these shoes as a joke going away present, because his family runs the bowling alley there. I had to promise I would wear them my first day here, so I did. I have gotten dirty looks from three teachers so far. Of course I have been trying to find a blue and red bowling bag to match. Today after school you have got to show me some of the stores you were talking about, Steve."

"Okay, sure," I replied.

Greg seemed serious about wanting to go check out the greater Delacourte thrift scene, so just before the bell rang I called Mom and told her I had promised to show a new friend around town.

"No problem," she said. "I will tell your father you can't work tonight, just make sure you finish your homework, okay? Oh and Steven I would like to meet your new friend sometime if that's alright--have fun."

The whole conversation left me wondering why Mom was always so helpful when I tried to make new friends. Did she not like the ones I currently had? Was she feeling guilty about her parenting skills, or was she just trying to be a good mom? Oh well, at least for once I wouldn't have to worry about dealing with loading up a shitload of unwieldy boxes after school.

Later that day I found myself at Highland Thrift with not only Greg, but also Dave, Ron, Joey, and Stuart who for some reason had decided to tag along. Funny, my friends never ever came anywhere I wanted them to, but with a snap of his fingers they were following Greg like a couple of lost puppy dogs. They had known him what--four hours?

It had been so long since I had gone thrifting with my friends, I had forgotten how suffocating they could be. Stuart was loudly mocking a large green lamp and snorting, all the while knowing full well that we had a similar lamp in our living room. Though I had never noticed it before that day, more and more of the furnishings for sale looked like stuff at my house. No doubt it had been top of the line in 1974, but now it looked heavy, shabby and seriously outdated. I had wanted to invite Greg over, but what would he think? No doubt his house was full of the type of retro furnishings that would fetch top dollar at auctions, not twenty five bucks on sale at the local Goodwill.

Feeling somewhat dejected, I made my way over to the records hoping for a killer score, or at least something halfway decent to get my mind off of Stuart. (God, why were we even still friends with him?) As usual I had no luck whatsoever. The selection was typical for Highland, consisting mainly of obscure sixties easy listening bands and some *Sing Along with Mitch* albums similar to what my Great Aunt Erma owned. I wondered who the hell Mitch was and if he was a millionaire.

I jerked my head upwards as I heard a loud snort. Behind me, Stuart was holding up some sixties album whose cover featured a buxom blonde, complete with a beehive hairstyle, wearing a chartreuse bikini made up of an extreme amount of extra fabric compared to today's standards.

"Oh-La-La, I think I should buy this one for the cover alone," he said in this voice that I guess was supposed to sound like James Bond or something.

"Do it, Do it--it's only like fifty cents. Hey do you think this place has got some vintage *Playboys* somewhere?" Joey said egging him on.

"I hope so 'cause I really wanna see your mom" Dave said loudly, thus causing everyone else in the store to turn their heads our way.

I could feel myself turning beet red. God, my friends were so immature. No doubt by this time Monday, Greg would have traded his bowling shoes in for 150 dollar Nikes and would be laughing with all the popular people about us losers, while Justine was perched on his arm ready to be swept off to the Junior Prom.

Chapter 8
Time to Take a U-Haul to Your Life!

Later that day I was still fuming. It was no wonder my friends were not popular, they acted like they were still ten. Every time we had the slightest bit of opportunity to get noticed, they would somehow blow it. Half the school was going to be at Sam Lauer's keg party tomorrow night and as usual my friends and I would be at one of our houses eating Cheetos, drinking sodas, and watching some stupid karate video. I might as well start hanging out with all the role playing geeks.

I threw myself down on one of our blue seventies era couches. I swear our living room set looked even worse than the ones at Goodwill, and courtesy of Oreo and Sanchez, they were covered in pet hair. My little sister Jeanne came in and once she saw that I was watching TV she started up her usual whining act. Once Jeanne starts up she can reach pitches that only a dog could hear.

"I was going to watch TV, I need to do my homework, I thought you were going to your friends, I was gonna invite all my annoying little friends over, I don't want you to have one moment of relaxation in your life ever--Maaaaa tell Steven to movit--he's not even watching anything--Maaaa!"

My mother would usually respond to this in her most annoyed tone:

"I have had a long day at work, the new filing system is confusing, the computer doesn't work, my new boss was looking at me crosseyed. There were tons of annoying students with no paperwork demanding financial aid in small unmarked bills...can't you two resolve anything yourselves ever?"

For some reason her built in mom radar perked up this time and she could sense I was in a very bad mood even though I hadn't opened my mouth or even moved.

"Jeanne can you do your homework upstairs, please? You can go watch my TV if you must. Steven, what's wrong?" she asked.

"Nothing," I grumbled.

"Are you sure you don't want to talk about it? Did you have a fight with your new friend?" she asked.

"No I'm fine," I responded, my vocal register climbing dangerously towards yell territory. Why couldn't people in this house leave me alone for five minutes? I reached over and un-muted the TV and stared randomly at a game show until she left to go cook dinner.

Of course I wasn't off the hook for that long and I knew it. I watched Jeopardy for half an hour until my father came over and sat down. As skilled at the storage space rental process as the man may be, Jack White had apparently secretly wanted to be a child psychologist. Dad always had a pat answer that probably came from some book like-*How to be Confident and Popular now! Ten strategies that will never work in the real world* or *Common sense ideas worded so confusingly you will never get past the first few pages! (A dynamic guide for self-starting proactive individuals who think outside the box)*

I could have chosen that moment to flee to my room in the guise of completing my homework, but that only meant he would corner me at work and I would end up talking about all my problems while loading up a space that probably belonged to the gossipy father of an even more gossipy popular kid.

So as usual for the sake of my privacy and to make him feel like the father of the year, I sat and listened to Dad.

"Your mother tells me you had a fight with your new friend," he said.

"No," I responded and glanced back at TV which was now playing *Wheel of Fortune*.

"Oh, then what's bugging you? Is it girl trouble?" he asked, letting out a giggle.

I glanced over at Dad, and judging from the fact that he was leaning back, legs crossed with a beer in one hand--I figured he wasn't going away anytime soon.

"No it's not girl trouble--with the friends I have, I pretty much don't have to worry about attracting girls ever," I said.

"Oh, so it's old friend trouble," he responded in that--I know all too well--voice of his. How could he possibly know? I have tried many times to imagine Dad my age, but all I can picture is the same slightly overweight middle age guy a bit shorter, with less gray in his hair and in fifties clothes.

If I cared that much I would go dig out a picture of him when he was a teenager. I don't think I have ever seen one, because they are all packed away somewhere in the attic, basement, or garage and when you deal with heavy, dusty boxes all the time the last thing you want to do on your day off is to sort through and deal with more heavy, dusty boxes.

"So come on Steven, why don't you tell me what your friends did this time?" Dad continued.

I sighed and explained what happened earlier that day and how lately they were getting more and more on my nerves. "But hey," I went on "Mom should be happy, I mean I don't think she likes any of my friends that well."

"Your mother likes your friends just fine--don't use her as an excuse. It sounds like you have just been around them too much lately. I think you should try to spend a couple of days where you don't hang out after school. Then I'm sure you'll find things are better."

Okay Dad, whatever, you just want me to spend more time around here so I will end up doing all the work. Maybe you are the one I need to take a vacation from.

"It's not just that I'm around them too much, but all the girls I like only want to be with popular guys. They never notice me and my friends or when they do it's usually for something embarrassing," I said, then shifted my weight on our ancient lumpy couch cushions. "Today at lunch we ate with Greg and suddenly all the popular people were noticing us and saying what's up and stuff. Anyway, I thought I finally had a chance at getting this girl, Justine to notice me, but of course two seconds later the rest of my friends started acting like completely immature dorks as usual. I'm sure Greg will never want to hang out with me again after today."

By now my father was relishing his opportunity to play amateur Freud. He uncrossed his legs, cleared his throat and prepared to set me straight.

"So the new friend you are talking about is Greg huh? The same Greg whose father rented number twenty nine, right?" he asked.

"Yup," I said.

"He seemed like a nice enough kid to me. Did it ever occur to you that the reason why you perceive Greg to be so popular is because he doesn't obsess over little things like what people think of him? Maybe he thought your friends were funny. The reason why people become popular is because they are relaxed and confident about themselves instead of always being so concerned about what other people think. To tell the truth I thought you were more like that, after all you never seem to care about what people think of your rather unique shopping habits, not to mention your taste in music and clothing."

Dad paused for a second to take a sip of his beer then continued, "Listen to me Steven, believe it or not I was once your age, and I know how much you want to be considered popular, but being a member of that crowd is definitely not what it's cracked up to be. Often the harder you try to be the center of attention the less popular you actually become. Think about your friend Stuart, he always tries to get noticed by making up outrageous lies, or spending too much money on clothes, but he often comes off as annoying, doesn't he? Don't get me wrong, I like Stuart. He's a good kid but he tries too hard. Just relax. If this Justine is worthy of you she will like you for yourself okay. Now if you don't mind it smells like the lasagna is almost done and I am really hungry."

He got up and walked towards the kitchen and I followed wondering if he memorized Brady Bunch episodes while I was at school or something. Amazingly, I felt better after our chat though I had no idea why. If it was so darn easy to be relaxed and confident, sure of yourself and all that other crap, then wouldn't Tony Robbins be working at the local Seven Eleven? Maybe my father should tour the country as a motivational speaker. He could use the whole storage industry as a metaphor: Remember you have to lock away all the bad memories in a storage space-lock them away and walk away-It's time to take a U-Haul to your life!

The man thinks it is so easy to be popular only because he is originally from some small town in Oregon no one has ever heard of. If you are in a graduating class of twenty it's easy to stand out and be the big fish, it's just too bad my high school class is made up of almost 500 people. If a young Jack White were to travel through time and try to navigate the bustling halls and overly defined social structure of Delacourte High, he wouldn't last a day.

I decided that I simply felt better because my mom makes really good lasagna. Who needs friends when you can eat some lasagna made with a hearty meat sauce and about fourteen types of cheese?

Chapter 9
Friendships, Advice, and Hot Dogs with No Buns

Much to my amazement Greg Lewis had not left our little group by Monday--in fact he actually seemed to be closer to my friends.

"Dude where were you Friday night?" Dave asked me at lunch. "We watched *Caddyshack*-it was hella funny."

Holy crap--they had actually watched a movie without Kung-Fu elements and I had missed it all due to following my father's dopey advice of creating some space. Oh well, I had seen *Caddyshack* approximately four hundred times anyway.

"Oh umm sorry, I had this stomach bug, but I'm doing better now. Just in time for school huh?" I shrugged in response.

Greg was leaning back watching a group of popular kids who in turn all seemed to be watching Matt Kingsley play hackey sack with his eyes closed.

"Popular people are so boring," he announced.

I looked over at Kingsley's fanclub before returning my gaze back towards Greg. Was he completely insane? Did he not hear about Sam's keg party? I had been jealously eavesdropping on the popular crowd's weekend exploits all morning. Kelly Rand's detailed expose of how Jenny Hudson had passed out behind two garbage cans into a pile of freshly raked leaves was far more interesting than the boring tape we were supposed to be listening to in French. When the recorded voice told me to *ecoutez bien*--listen well--I did. Just not to him.

"What are you smoking?" I asked Greg. "When you are popular you can go to all the cool parties, and date the best looking chicks just because you can play basketball or some shit. What's boring about that?"

"Trust me, about two years ago I was one of them," Greg said. "I was always worried about if I was wearing the right shirt, or going out with the right girl, or listening to the right band. The whole point of being popular is to make everybody envy you, but you get so caught up in making sure people are jealous that you are not having any fun. Your hot girlfriend is just dating you to make the other chicks jealous and you are only still dating her to make the other guys jealous because you found out a long time ago that she is just boring man. You end up hanging out at the mall and sitting outside a dressing room at the Gap on like all of your dates."

"Yeah that sucks," Joey agreed.

"Oh and if your best friend was in band all of a sudden you can't be friends in school anymore cause he's a band geek," Greg continued. "It's like this at every school I have ever been to. When they get old all those people over there are going to realize that they just thought they were cool-but the real cool people were those who had it figured out man. The real cool people are us. We are not all into impressing people. We just want to have fun right?"

"Oh yeah man totally," Stuart grinned and shook his head.

I am pretty sure that this would be the first and only time anyone would ever classify Stuart Meeley as cool. I didn't have the heart to remind any of my friends that for a crowd that just wanted to have fun-we seemed to rent an awful lot of videos. Instead I got up and headed over to my locker.

Greg stopped me just as I started to put my backpack on. "Hey I gotta get something from our space tonight so maybe I will see you after school," he said. "Plus I want to ask you something."

"Okay, see ya," I said.

...

I was tossing a basketball into the net located against the end wall of our largest lockers when Greg stopped by.

"Hey what's up? Hard at work or hardly working?" he asked.

Like I had never heard that one before.

"Business is slow, so what are you gonna do," I said chasing after the basketball which had completely missed the net as usual. "Can you get in your space okay or did you lose the key?"

"Nope I got it. I just heard the ball and thought I'd say hey." he said. "My dad threw out his back moving stuff at the restaurant and his massage pad is in the space. I gotta go fish it out."

I found myself watching him sort through boxes and making small talk, not sure if he was paying attention or not.

"My dad throws out his back a lot. I guess it's one of the perils of owning a storage place. Anyway he probably knows a good chiropractor. If you want I can ask."

Greg didn't seem to hear my chiropractor advice instead he yelled. "I got it" and stepped out of the space holding up some sort of a rolled up mat with an electrical cord dangling from it.

"Hey Steve, you got anything to drink?" Greg Asked after he tossed the mat in his trunk.

"Sure, you want a soda? My treat." Greg looked at me weird.

"I have to buy it from the machine. My mom doesn't like us to have soda in our fridge so every time I want one I have to buy it," I said as we walked over to the vending machine. My Dad has the key. I think it's how he gets back my allowance."

Greg decided on Coke and took a look at the machine.

"Why is it right in front of this locker?" He asked.

"This one's door is busted so we don't use it plus it's close to a plug," I said.

"Don't you think that's weird, though? I mean this locker looks fine to me."

I looked over at the door, Greg was right it really didn't look that bad. "I guess most of the dent is behind the machine," I said. "You said you wanted to ask me something?"

"Actually I need to ask your dad something. Is he around?" Greg said.

"He went to the office supply store but he should be back pretty soon if you want to wait around." I responded.

My father was forever going to hardware stores and office supply places in the guise of keeping the Stor'N'More well stocked. We never seemed to be low on tape rolls and the knife inserts we sold in the office, but that didn't stop him. I assumed that he just used them as an excuse to make a pit stop at one of the plethora of donut shops, ice cream places, and bakeries located within Delacourte's city limits.

Mom was forever buying Nutra-grain bars, rice cakes, and diet fruit punch, with the hope that for once someone other than herself would reach for something healthy. Deep down, I suspected she always knew it was a lost cause. Wahl's drug was conveniently located on the way to school and had been fulfilling my sucrose needs since the first day of freshman year. Jeanne had a large network of friends who supported her habit in exchange for homework help and Dad's wallet was overflowing with buy five get one free punch cards from the Delacourte Confectionery Company.

...

Greg agreed to stick around until Dad returned, so he followed me into the house and upstairs to my room, where I self-consciously felt his eyes wander around. They glanced past the Ricky Stevenson posters, my outdated computer, the shabby dresser where Sanchez Tabby sat licking his paws, and landed on my bright blue electric guitar, and it's portable amplifier.

"Sweet guitar, you play?" He asked and I nodded.

"Yeah the guys told me you are into Ricky Stevenson. Can you play surf rock on that thing?"

"A little bit but I can't right now because I have to be able to hear if the bell rings downstairs." I said. "What about you? Do you play an instrument?"

"I have an old acoustic guitar of my dad's," he said "but I have no idea how to play it. Do you teach people?"

"I am still taking lessons myself," I responded. "There are a lot of classes at the music store. You should sign up for one of those"

"Maybe," he said then abruptly changed the subject to the conversation we had held earlier that day.

"You've got pretty cool taste, Steve; I can't believe you want to be popular. They've all got terrible taste, I heard at Kingsley's party Saturday night all they played was rap. Plus you wouldn't look like Ricky Stevenson if you went all preppy like them."

I wondered why Greg had become some sort of missionary trying desperately to steer me away from the evils of the popular lifestyle. It's not like they were sending me engraved invitations that read: Dear Steven J. White Esq.; Matthew Kingsley and the other members of the most exclusive popular group sometimes referred to as the "in crowd" would like your presence at their lunch table and various social events. Please R.S.V.P. Immediately.

"Dude," I said. "I never said I wanted to *be* popular. I just want to date a certain popular girl and get invited to more parties. I am not going to run down and buy some eighty dollar sweatshirt and sit on the other side of the cafeteria hoping everyone in the popular crowd will suddenly notice me."

"Oh okay I didn't mean to offend you, I am just saying high school popularity is overrated in general. Wait, which girl do you like?" He asked.

Damn Greg, way to pry. "Oh just this girl, Justine. I mean I don't really know her that well or anything, it's just she is really pretty. I probably have zero chance anyway since I heard she likes Matt Kingsley." I told him, regretting it seconds later as usual. Why oh why do I reveal so much to other people anyway?

"Oh Justine, yeah I think I know who you mean, she's kinda quiet right? She is really pretty, but I don't really know her either. I was thinking you were going to say Kelly Rand. She is in that crowd, but I swear she is just itching to rebel. By next year she will have gone punk or something. She just needs someone to point her in a new direction and hopefully it will be me," Greg said giving me a wink.

Kelly Rand--could he be any less original? Kelly's supposed lusciousness dominated most of my tables' conversation every lunchtime. Sure she was pretty in that generic cheerleader way and would definitely do in a pinch, but the fact remains Kelly Rand comes nowhere near Justine Weeks territory on the hotness scale.

"So you like Kelly. Dave has been in love with her since kindergarten, and I know Stuart likes her too, not that he has a chance. Kelly seems nice enough I guess, but she is no Justine." I told Greg just before our conversation was abruptly ended by the telltale slam of our front door.

Judging by the loud clatter of screen door and front door colliding and separating I could tell this was the work of my father. Jeanne could never get such great door acoustics and my mother had never ever slammed a door in her life.

"Hey Mr. White," Greg said after we located Dad downstairs in the Stor'N'More office. "My father's restaurant is opening soon and he wanted me to you let you know that we are having a pre-opening party next Saturday at five and your family is invited. Anyway he would have invited you himself but he threw out his back and is trying to take it easy for a few days. Anyway hope to see you guys there, I gotta go." He then went outside and hopped on a restored blue and white Schwinn from the fifties.

I half expected a gloating speech about how successful the other night's father-son talk had been, but Dad only said,

"Interesting kid, I haven't seen a bike like that since I was your age."

...

A couple of hours later I got tired of aimlessly flipping through the channels on my TV while I put off my homework so I ventured toward the kitchen in order to investigate what was for dinner that night. As it always is in our family, I ran into a complication long before I reached my intended destination.

This time it was my mother and she must have had an unpleasant day at work. For the most part, Ellen White is an agreeable woman. She is willing to put up with a house on the wrong end of town, long lines of irritated university students, an underachieving son, a daughter with expensive taste in clothing, and a husband who refuses to follow her dietary advice. Every once in a while it occurs to my mother just how annoying these things are and she gets in one of her moods. I tried to avoid Mom like I always do when she is grouchy, but she was blocking my path.

"Steven James White, how many times have I told you to stop leaving these guitar things around?" She announced.

Guitar things? What exactly did that mean? God forbid my mother should ever say the actual name of something.

Avoiding more eye contact, I instead looked down at her hands. The left one was holding one of my picks.

"It wasn't me I swear. Every time I play my guitar I put the pick back into the Yellowstone mug on my desk. Honest. Go take a look; I have like ten in there. Someone else must be going through my stuff. I bet it was Jeanne," I responded.

I know I sounded defensive but everything I said was true. Lately I had been making the effort to really put my picks away, not because I was becoming a neat freak by any stretch of the imagination, but because Richardson's Music had stopped giving them away free with every purchase.

"This was right smack in the middle of the coffee table along with a bunch of other junk, and don't give me that--it must be Jeanne--crap mister. You know full well that you are the only one who plays a guitar here."

I could see I wasn't going to gain any ground, but that didn't stop me. Within the few short seconds after Mom's revelation, I had convinced myself that Jeanne spent her afternoons dragging my guitar all over the house, tossing it out windows, breaking the strings, playing with all the knobs till they came loose, and purposely trying to blow out my amplifier. So I looked Mom directly in the eye and announced:

"I haven't played my guitar anywhere besides my room in ages. In fact I can't even remember the last time I played here in the den."

"What about the other day when you had your friends over and you were showing off that new song you learned?" She said.

Shit, she had me there. Isn't age seventeen a little young for Alzheimer's to be setting in? I could have sworn I put back the pick when I took my guitar and amp upstairs. When Mom got done yelling at me I would have to run back upstairs and make sure each and every knob and switch on Lu Lu Belle were exactly where I left them, or else my sister was going to pay.

"Uhhh, sorry, it won't happen again," I mumbled back at Mom. "What's for dinner anyway?"

"Talk to your father or Jeanne. I've been at work all day," was all she said.

Great. The only thing in the kitchen Jeanne could do was reheat macaroni and cheese leftovers until they were inedible rubbery goo. Attempting a new batch of Kraft dinner was way above her expertise. As far as my father went, anytime that man gets within a yard of the stove it is really best to have the local fire marshal standing by. It looked like we were going to have yet another wholesome family meal of Top Ramen a'la Steven. Perhaps I would add little chunks of lunchmeat for protein.

I walked into our--still stuck in the seventies--kitchen with its avocado green oven, and opened up all of our dark stained wood cabinets. None of them contained any sort of ramen, or even a lone cup-o-noodles. When we finally all sat down to eat our dinner of chopped up hot dogs with no buns, I wished Greg's father's dinner party was that night, instead of the following week.

Chapter 10
Hob Nobbing With The Elite

Downtown Delacourte is one of those places that seem tailor made for various university brochures featuring photos of students drinking coffee at one of its sidewalk cafes, or walking their bikes along its tree lined streets. It has been featured in several travel magazines with headlines like *The Midwest's most bicycle friendly town, A return to the downtown tradition,* and *Small town charm, big city culture.* The streets are filled with boutique-y clothing stores, overpriced designer outdoorsy sporting goods places and various other emporiums selling overpriced useless knick-knacks, like duck windchimes and personalized doormats. Most of the shops don't last that long but when they are replaced it is always with a store that is almost exactly the same. Last year Kelly's Kountry Charms gave way to Eleanor's Handcrafted Gifts Boutique, which had recently gone out of business. The old Eleanor's sign was now covered up by a banner that read: Coming Soon: Bettie's Beads Emporium.

Every full time resident of Delacourte soon learns that downtown is where you take the visitors for some food and a lovely stroll, but is pretty much impractical for everything else.

The night of Mr. Lewis' dinner party my father circled the block five times, as he tried to avoid the paying for the twenty-four hour parking garage. As we circled the downtown radius, I looked around at the many shops. I always feel sorry for the people who own them, because most people in this town (and probably most towns for that matter) do hardly any of their actual shopping here.

Instead everyone ventures to the south end of town where the mall, the Walmart and most of the nationwide chain restaurants are located. Not that I blame most people for shopping at all those stores. They probably just think; well I believe in supporting the little guy but I am on a budget right now, once I become a millionaire I will definitely only shop downtown.

My father finally gave in and parked in the garage as usual and we all piled out and headed down Main until we reached the restaurant, which was named TroPiCo. Either Greg had been misinformed or the whole sixties tropical-tiki look with a tongue in cheek flair had been thrown out the window at the last minute, because TroPiCo looked pretty much like most of the restaurants that had sprung up around the university lately chasing after some invisible yuppie demographic. It was done up mostly in a dark wood scheme with tan and green walls. The only thing vaguely tropical I saw were some artificial potted palms and bamboo trees placed here and there.

The party itself was actually more of an extended dinner featuring the movers and shakers of Delacourte, Indiana. (You know you are at a happening shindig when you are brushing elbows with Jack R. White: storage magnate, and his lovely wife Ellen.) The room was filled with an eclectic bunch of people that Greg and his father had met in the few short weeks they had been here, alongside those who Dan had known growing up in Delacourte. Carpet layers, plumbers, and electricians were seated next to various doctors, lawyers, and university bigwigs.

"Look Jack, it's Carl Evans, the Vice Provost of economic affairs." My mother was whispering to my father who turned to her and said

"Ellen look, there's Dr. Martin. It looks like Dan took me up on that recommendation. I hope his back is better."

I sat back and as I absorbed the conversation going around me, I wondered just what the hell is a Vice Provost anyway? It's one of those positions that sounds super important yet no one actually knows what they do. He probably sits back in his office wearing an expensive suit and doing nothing but thinking I can't believe they hired me to be a Provost man--it's like they don't know that provost is a totally made up position, ha ha ha suckers...

The main course was grilled salmon. Since my prior experience with salmon was the pink canned glop Mom used to make croquettes, I didn't know it could be so delicious. Everyone at our table seemed to be enjoying it immensely except for Jeanne who kept picking at hers and shifting her eyes around looking for various ways to escape.

"Da-ad you know I don't like fish it's so gross. I don't get why I had to come to this, there is nobody here my own age anyway. Mo-omm can I go next door and get a frozen yogurt?" she whined.

Mom handed my sister a couple of bucks probably just to be rid of her for a few minutes and within seconds Jeanne flew out the door barely yelling thanks.

Greg and his dad spent most of the party going from table to table, mingling with each of the guests. They stopped by our table shortly after we had finished with dessert. Mr. Lewis told us the story of why they had moved back to Delacourte, which was his hometown. They had been living in L.A. when Greg's mother left Dan, and the restaurant he was a chef at went under. They moved back to Indiana to save money, and Dan started a reasonably successful restaurant in Monroeville, a small town located about an hour away from here. Last year Mr. Lewis sold that restaurant because he had grown tired of the small town lifestyle of Monroeville, and he had hoped that his hometown's larger population would enable him to be more culinary adventurous.

"So Steven," Mr. Lewis said after he finished the story. "What do you think of TroPiCo? I am thinking of making the salmon my signature dish."

"The salmon was fantastic," I responded, "but the way Greg described it, I thought there were going to be more Tiki gods and stuff."

"Ah yes, that would have been concept A," Mr. Lewis said. "The space we have here just didn't feel right. The architecture was from the wrong era, there was too much brick, and we don't really have the space, so I decided it should be understated instead. Perhaps someday I will have an over the top ode to the rat pack era, just not right now. Maybe if I ever make it back to the west coast, it would be fun to bring back the glory days of The Tropical Trader."

"The Trader was really something wasn't it?" my father said. "I went there a couple of times when I was staying with a friend in the early 60's. That was some show, especially the indoor volcano. I wonder what the overhead on a place like that would be today."

"Yeah I am pretty sure it's a lot," Mr. Lewis remarked. "Maybe that's why I keep putting my version off. So did you ever see anyone famous while you ate at the *Trader*? I saw Barbara Eden once shortly before the place closed for good. At least I think it was Barbara Eden, she's hard to recognize without the genie outfit."

"Nope--none that I can recall, but it was usually pretty dark in there. I could have been sitting next to Elvis for all I know," my father said.

"Or more likely Ricky Stevenson, he ate there a lot they say," Mr. Lewis said glancing towards me. "Actually the only place I saw him was here. He played the University Quad in '61 I think it was, put on quite a show. I wonder what ever happened to him."

Mr. Lewis paused for a second then asked

"Say did you happen to keep any of your souvenirs? There is quite a collectible market for anything from that era-

-but especially if it's from the *Trader*. I wish I would have had the foresight to swipe an ashtray or two."

My father chuckled and said "Oh who knows? It's a proven fact that storage industry professionals are without a doubt the least organized people on the face of the earth. Though I might have something up in the attic in a box next to my Stradivarius."

Chapter 11
West Coast Dreams

"Dan is quite an interesting guy" my father said as we walked around the corner to the parking garage. "Though how he survived life in Monroeville is beyond me."

I had been wondering that myself since the only things Monroeville had going for it were a family style buffet and its location next to the interstate so you could easily get away from Monroeville.

"Who knows?" my mother said. "People's lives always seem to take unexpected turns."

"That's for sure," Dad agreed.

On the way back to parking garage we found Jeanne who had located a group of her friends at the Yogurt Palace and was busy playing some pinball.

"See, that wasn't so bad after all was it?" Dad asked her. "I could hardly pull you away from that quarter sucking game."

"I wasn't sucking up quarters. I am good at pinball. Can we go get a burger or something? I'm hecka starved," was her response.

"No, you should have eaten your salmon--that would have been a very expensive meal if we had to pay for it." Dad told her.

"If we had paid I wouldn't have ordered the salmon--I hate fish," Jeanne grumbled then slumped into the back seat of our dingy white station wagon with its faded Stor'N'More logo painted on the doors.

I think the rationale behind having the logo on the car is to give potential customers the powerful subliminal advertising message of *please please store your belongings at the Stor'N'More so its owners can afford a decent car someday.*

"Dad how come you never told us you used to live in L.A.?" I asked.

Seconds later, Jeanne piped in

"Dad lived in LA?"

"I never lived in LA, I just stayed there with a friend for a few weeks, while I checked out potential franchise opportunities," he said.

"How come you didn't stay?" Jeanne asked. It seemed she had forgotten she was angry at him for not getting her a burger.

"It would probably be a lot cooler to live there than here. They've got the beach and Disneyland. Did you go to Disneyland?"

"Yes I went to Disneyland once. It's just like a smaller Disney World don't tell me you have forgotten all about your trip to Disney World. You kids are getting spoiled," Dad grumbled, but I wasn't going to let him change the subject so easily.

"Yeah Dad" I said "How come you didn't stay in LA longer? Didn't you like it?"

"It's not that I didn't like it, I was just checking things out. LA was a very expensive place to live even then and besides, if I had settled in LA I wouldn't have met your mother and you two would not even exist."

When the car rolled into our driveway (actually the gated entrance to the Stor'N'More) Jeanne and I gave each other secretive sibling glances. Without uttering a word these glances announced: we have just found out about a part of one of our parents' lives we didn't previously know about, and we must get as much info as possible before Dad retires to the master bedroom upstairs. I will guard the stairs while you try to corner him in the front hallway.

Dad struggled getting our door open as usual. The man is very handy when it comes to keeping the office and the majority of the lockers in tip top shape, but as soon as you cross the threshold from business to residence everything pretty much falls apart. Finally the door heaved open and we rushed inside to avoid the evening's chill. Dad started to hang up his coat on the rack and I took it to be a perfect time to continue the conversation.

"So Dad, when you stayed in LA who did you stay with? Does he still live there?" I asked.

Dad grumbled something about it being a long day and needing to go upstairs but he could tell by the way Jeanne and I were standing; with both pairs of feet planted firmly in front of his path, that we were not going to go away anytime soon.

So he muttered. "I stayed with Stan Johnson, you don't know him. We sort of lost touch over the years, it happens. Why are you so interested anyway?"

It was a good question. Why were we so interested? I guess it's just because the concept of parents having one shred of privacy is inherently offensive to their offspring, so we pressed on.

"We just want to see Los Angeles, Dad. It's got to be more interesting than here," I said. "What part of L.A. does your friend live in?" Jeanne piped in before Dad had a chance to respond. "Do you think he still lives there? Does he know any famous people?"

"L.A. is not that interesting kids," he said. "It's like everywhere else. It has some areas that are nice and others that are not. It's very expensive, and most of it's a desert so everything's very dry. I don't know any famous people personally, but I have heard that for the most part they are spoiled jerks." Dad paused a second but we were still blocking the stairs so he continued.

"We could go there on vacation, is that what you want Steven? I will take you to Panorama City which is the part I stayed in, and I guarantee within a couple of days both of you will want to be back here where the grass is lush, there is no smog, and the people are nice. Now if you don't mind I am exhausted and I am going to bed. Good night." With that he brushed us aside and marched up the stairs.

"Panorama City--do you know what part of LA that's in?" Jeanne asked me. "I bet it's got great views."

"I have no idea-Ricky Stevenson never lived in a place called Panorama City. Maybe tomorrow I will buy a map of LA and try to find it," I told her.

Chapter 12
A Rousing Game of Piss Off Steve

A late October chill had set over the city of Delacourte, which meant snow was probably just around the corner. When snow falls here it follows a pattern. If you are driving through the university or downtown it looks fresh and clean like a postcard, but once you hit our part of town it has turned to a sheet of hard crunchy ice dirtied by the cars going down Highland, as well as by the general griminess of this side of town. Jeanne and I learned early on that a snowball fight at home usually consists of more pain than fun so we would save the urges to hurl projectile objects until the occasional days when one of our parents would take us over to the local park.

Maybe if there is an early snow Jeanne and I could talk Mom and Dad into taking a trip to LA. Jeanne wants to see Disneyland, the beach, and hopefully some movie stars, while I have always wanted to go and see where Ricky Stevenson lived.

Not that I had any plans to tell Dad the real reason I wanted to visit Southern California. My father thinks my fascination with Ricky is a phase I should have already passed out of. Usually adults think my affliction is harmless or even cute. (well at least Mom thinks it's cute), but not Dad. When Greg's father introduced me as Delacourte

Indiana's answer to Ricky Stevenson at his party most of the adults present chuckled and murmured something about an uncanny resemblance to Ricky. Dad, however, made a clenching grimace, and tried to change the subject.

I never quite understood why the man doesn't approve. Liking Ricky Stevenson is not something I am doing because I know he's not a fan. If I wanted to infuriate Dad I would listen to heavy metal, rap, or go to raves. Instead I listen to someone from his generation. I imagine most parents would be ecstatic about this, but not my father, no of course not. Does the man even listen to music? His side of the stereo cabinet is mostly classical, while mom's collection of old Beatles albums take up most of the shelves.

When I did my speech on Ricky Stevenson--which got me an A by the way--he groused.

"Why are you doing your report on a dead rock and roll star, instead of someone who made an impact in this world? What kind of school lets it students do reports on anything?"

Since when does choosing a career dealing with the storage of people's excess belongings qualify one as an intellectual snob, I wondered. Oh please Father, direct me towards your Ph.D. in Storology.

So I had to explain "It's not a report--it's a speech, and people do better on speeches about subjects they know about. I know about Ricky Stevenson. If I do a speech on him I will get an A; if I do a speech on Beethoven or somebody I will get a C-. Which would you rather I get an A or a C? I need to get more A's aren't you always saying that? Anyway I still have plenty of other reports and stuff to do on important people."

Fortunately Mom often stood up for me when Dad grumbled.

"Jack" she would say. "Why are you criticizing Steven? It's just a hobby. I would much rather he was into oldies than some of that music the kids listen to these days. I hear it blasting every time I walk past the dorms on my way to lunch, and most of it seems to be about shooting people and doing drugs. Is that what you want Steven to be into?"

"Of course I don't want Steven to do drugs. I just think he should start paying more attention to his school subjects. He will be a senior next year, then what? Where is he going to college? Do we even know that yet? Or is Steven's grand plan to dress up as Ricky Stevenson, move to New York and play guitar for the people getting off the subway?"

Eventually however Dad would mellow out and do his best to ignore my vintage shirts and gelled hair, and I did my best to not bring up any Ricky related subjects unless they were pertinent to the conversation.

...

My father was not the only person who didn't quite comprehend my love for all things Ricky Stevenson. Whenever my friends got bored one of them would invariably start up their favorite game: Piss Off Steve. The rules to Piss Off Steve are simple, to play you simply start up a familiar conversation about music in general and guitarists in particular. During this conversation you must be sure to unfavorably compare the guitar playing of Ricky Stevenson to Jimi Hendrix, Carlos Santana, Eddie Van Halen or whoever is the hottest guitar player currently ruling the radio. By doing this you will have reached your goal. You will have pissed off Steve. (There is a more extreme version of this game in which you unfavorably compare the guitar playing of Ricky Stevenson to John Denver or any of The Monkees, but I don't recommend playing this version if you would like to continue being my friend after the conversation ends.)

When it comes to playing Piss Off Steve, Joey was the worst offender. Everyone knows at least one person who instinctively knows all the buttons to push to make a guy go crazy, and for me that person is Joey Hertz. He relishes in the torture of relatives, teachers, and especially his friends. When my other friends would talk about music, I knew I was probably safe but when Joey started, I would instinctively brace myself for an unprovoked tirade against all the things I hold dear.

"Hey Steve," he began. "I just got the new Intrepid Burglars CD, and wow that Monty Turner sure can wail. You should go pick it up. Hear what a real guitarist sounds like."

"Shut up Joey."

"Not like that fifties crap you always listen to."

"Seriously Joey--shut up. I am not in the mood for this."

Joey turned to Dave, (for some reason he always turned to Dave) and said,

"Dave you should go out and get the album. I know you can appreciate a good guitar solo. Trust me, you will really like it. Monty is good. He's not Hendrix good, but he's getting close."

"I am really short on cash Joey; can't I just make a tape off you?" Dave asked.

'Sure," Joey responded. "It's good to know that I have at least one friend who has the sense to know what a guitar should sound like."

At this point I started to crack. I know I should just keep my big mouth shut and hope the conversation fades but I can't. Joey doesn't know shit about music and I can't stand the idea of anyone thinking he does, so I interrupted him and let the debate get underway.

"Joey."

"What?"

"I never said Monty Turner wasn't a good guitarist. He's okay but face it Monty Turner comes nowhere close to the standard that Ricky Stevenson set."

"Standard, come on Steven, what are you high? Ricky Stevenson was a cheesy teen idol who occasionally strummed a guitar. The only reason why people even remember him today is because he disappeared. I mean excuse me, but I don't think Van Halen ever played a song with tambourines in the background."

"Ricky played in the early sixties. Every song back then had a tambourine in it. If Guns and Roses was around back then every song they played would have had tambourines in the background and girls singing backup. You can't compare Ricky to the guitar style of today, that's not fair. You have to compare him to the era. Ricky Stevenson was way ahead of the curve for 1964. He was an innovator. You have probably never really listened to Ricky and the Sleepers. Hearing a muzak version of Lanie, Lanie in the mall doesn't count," I took a second to catch my breath and noticed that Joey still had an annoying smirk.

"Serious musicians love Ricky," I continued. "All the best guitarists of today always cite him as one of their influences. My guitar teacher loves Ricky, and I don't know anyone who knows more about music than him. His boss likes Ricky and the Sleepers too. Why do you think there is that huge poster of Ricky over the guitar section? If Ricky was still playing today he would just blow the competition away," I stood up and grabbed my backpack.

"I don't make fun of what you guys listen to so why do you always give me crap about what I like? I am sick of this. From here on out I am not ever going to have a conversation about Ricky Stevenson with people who listen to Milli Vanilli or *The Humpty Dance*," I swung the pack over my shoulders and decided to finish my lunch elsewhere.

I knew I wouldn't stick to my threat to never speak to my friends about music ever again. It was too much of a major part of my existence. Sometimes I felt like a modern ambassador of Ricky's sound. Since the world's best guitarist is no longer around to represent himself someone had to, and I just knew I would eventually be able to get my friends to appreciate his music. Even the friends who were named Joey.

Maybe they would get more excited about Ricky if I told them about how great his hometown was. Since the night we ate at TroPiCo Jeanne was convinced we would visit L.A. during our Christmas vacation. I was not so hopeful about this trip actually taking place. Dad was being pretty sarcastic that night and I couldn't believe that Jeanne the family "brain" didn't notice this. Perhaps, I could up our chances of a Southern California visit by telling Mom and Dad I wanted to tour UCLA, and other colleges in the LA area.

When I got home from school I shirked my office duty and went up to my room. I had purchased a map of Southern California the other day and posted it onto my bulletin board. I had already placed blue pins in all the places Ricky had lived and a green pin in Panorama City which seemed pretty close to Van Nuys, where Ricky had grown up. I grabbed a couple of yellow pins and stuck one in UCLA and the other on USC. Unfortunately neither seemed to be anywhere within the vicinity of Van Nuys and Panorama City, if we did end up going to LA I would have to figure out some other excuse to get them to visit those cities.

Chapter 13
Halloween Plans

October was ending quickly, and for the first time in my entire life I realized I had no plans for Halloween other than dressing up for school. I stopped dressing up as Ricky Stevenson every year because I practically look like him every day now. I retired Ricky as a costume after my freshman year because Dan Parker also went as Ricky Stevenson--only he went as Ricky after driving into the Mississippi river. Dan's Ricky impersonation included white zombie makeup, algae stapled to his shirt, ripped clothes, and a half a guitar. I acted offended, but secretly I thought it was hilarious.

Since Ricky was no longer an option, and I was Elvis last year, I decided to go as Michael Jackson. Thanks to the wonders of Highland Thrift official Halloween headquarters of the creative poor, I acquired one red vinyl jacket which I spray painted with glitter in a can, two white gloves (one would be left at home), funky black shoes, a working boombox, and a tape copy of *Bad*. (I looked and looked but I just couldn't find *Thriller*.)

There was no Halloween dance scheduled this year. This was due to what the leadership class deemed financial difficulties, though to me it appeared to be the age old tradition of failing to get ones shit together. I mean come on how hard is it to buy a couple of bags of orange and black M&M's, some crepe paper and one of those spooky sounds tapes they have at Wahl's Drugs for $5.99. There are plenty of students at this school under the delusion that they are D.J.s. I know they would work cheap-maybe even for free if they could get some extra credit.

I could just imagine Principal Derrick leaning back at his desk, confronting yet another hopeless case while our school secretary would stand behind him holding a yardstick ready to act as the "bad cop" should further action be needed.

Derrick would loudly crack his knuckles, clear his throat and announce:

"Mister Lennon, this F in History will not look very good on your permanent record, but maybe we can work out a deal. You play some non-offensive dance tracks that most of student body likes at the Halloween Party, and I will see about making that F magically turn into a C- How does that sound Tommy."

Of course I knew this would never happen. It is a well-known secret at almost every high school, and college that this sort of grade magic only happens when the participation in a sport is at stake. Football players get all the breaks, all the girls and most of the scholarships too.

As the calendar grew ever closer to the 31st the lack of Halloween activities were continually noted by my friends at lunch. I'm not sure why it was such a big deal to us, I mean since the eighth grade dance we have just not had that much fun, but still the thought of nothing to do was overly depressing.

"This sucks," I moaned. "I am going to run for leadership next year just to make sure this doesn't happen again."

"I heard that the leadership people have enough money but they are just using it all for themselves--like next week they are having this bowling party," Dave grumbled.

"I heard all the Goth kids are sacrificing a bird at the old VA hospital. Maybe we should join them." muttered Joey.

"Look Halloween is overrated anyway," Ron said. "Last year's dance was so dumb I should have just stayed home and passed out candy like I am going to do this year. I mean it's just one day so why are we stressing over it?"

I was more bummed that my other friends, At least they would have candy to pass out but no one ever trick or treated at our place seeing as how it is pretty much the only residence on Highland. Jeanne was going to her friend's Halloween party, so I would be the one stuck at home with Mom and Dad watching dumb horror movies from the fifties or a *Full House* Halloween episode or something. I wondered if the popular kids were having some sort of a gigantic Halloween keg party that I could sneak into, or maybe I could crash a college party.

Since I knew my father would never let me live if I did either, and the fact that parties where you know nobody else are even more depressing than staying at home I contemplated throwing a Halloween party of my own. Nothing fancy, just a basic excuse to eat pizza and watch movies, after all why should I waste a perfectly good Michael Jackson outfit?

...

"Hey Dave, got any plans for Halloween yet?" I asked the next day as we walked to French class.

"Just passing out candy, why?"

"I was thinking we all need to get together and do something. We can talk more at lunch when everybody's there."

"Yeah good idea, I mean I don't really want to pass out candy," he said.

When lunch came around I made my announcement.

"So, since none of us have any plans for Halloween, I think we should get together, maybe watch some horror videos or something, not a huge deal. If you want we can have it at my house or wherever."

"We should have it at my house," Greg said. "I was going to help my father scare kids at the door, you guys can help us then we can hang out. Plus I have been meaning to have a party one of these days, why not Halloween?"

"Okay that sound's great, I mean my house is kind of far from everyone else's," I said, slightly relieved. Nothing dampened a social event faster than the presence of Jack and Ellen White. It's not that I don't love my parents but they hover constantly. Mom at least disguises her intruding nature by spending her time in the kitchen making bizarre hors d'oeuvres that people my age would never eat. Dad makes no effort to hide the fact that he is keeping his eye on us. He is not only certain that my friends will consume every bit of alcohol in our house but he has convinced himself that they will make off with rolls of packing tape, file folders and mass quantities of bubble wrap from the Stor'N'More office.

Chapter 14
Goth Girls and Glitter Jackets

The closer you get to the university, the more pretentious the street names get. It's quite easy to find yourself completely lost in a neighborhood full of towering trees and large houses that were built around the 1930's and 40's trying desperately to remember if you turned on Shakespeare, Cervantes, or Balzac Avenue. Greg's house was in Hampton Commons, a small subdivision off Chaucer, one of the few sections featuring newer houses near the university.

I made my way up the path to their door and looked around. The Lewis's were apparently the type of people who went all out for Halloween. The yard had been strewn with cardboard tombstones, carved pumpkins, and that cottony fake cobweb stuff you can buy at the drugstore. I didn't have the heart to tell Mr. Lewis that probably not enough people had moved into the houses yet to make the effort worthwhile.

As I stepped closer, I noticed that the porch light had been replaced with a blacklite and they were playing a spooky sounds tape through a pair of speakers in the front window. I rang the bell and a few seconds later the door slowly opened to reveal a plywood coffin which slowly opened to reveal Mr. Lewis wearing a vampire cape holding a bowl of candy.

"Vould you like zome candy little boy?" Mr. Lewis quickly lost the lame faux vampire accent and started talking in his normal voice. "Come on in Steven looks like you're the first one here. Let me guess your Michael Jackson this year. I hate to break it to you but that nose looks way to real."

As I stepped inside he glanced down the street towards the Stormobile which I had driven. "Ooh, you should have told me you had a station wagon Steven. I could have done it up as a hearse. Oh well," he sighed.

Greg's house smelled of new carpet, and cardboard boxes, an odor you would think my nose would have become acclimated to by now. The outside had a fake colonial exterior but inside everything looked like it was from the 1950's and 60's. As I was glancing around the den Greg came up to me and started talking.

"My Dad collects furniture mostly from the fifties isn't that weird? I mean who collects furniture?" he asked.

"Greg you are talking to a guy who's obsessed with a missing rock star, nothing is weird to me," I said.

"I see your point," He continued. "Anyway some of the furniture is valuable, so we are having the party mostly in the basement. Dad still hasn't forgiven me for this one party I threw back in Monroeville. You bust one little Eames chair."

"What's an Aims Chair?" I interrupted

"The Eames were this couple that designed furniture back in the fifties. I guess I am around my dad so much that I forget that normal people don't know these things," he said. "Anyway, come on; let's go downstairs I'm starving."

The basement continued with the whole retro theme, but seemed to be a lot more relaxed than the white sparseness of the upstairs. Greg walked over to the corner of the room which had a bar done up tiki style, and started pouring something.

"Hey you want a beer? Just don't tell my Dad, okay? He's going to be busy with the trick or treaters for a while," he said.

All right, a beer, now he was talking, perhaps this party held more promise than I originally thought.

"Sure," I said, glancing back towards the stairwell. "Do you really think there will be that many trick or treaters? I mean this neighborhood doesn't look all that finished to me."

"My dad told all the people he knows with kids to come give us a visit. He really gets into holidays, as I'm sure you noticed." Greg said as he wrestled with a stubborn bag of party mix. "How's the beer? I know somebody with an older brother who got me a couple of cases. Don't worry about my dad; he usually doesn't intrude when I have people over."

The party soon got relatively busy and Mr. Lewis stayed upstairs for the most part popping in and out a couple of times until he came down one last time.

"I am going up to my room to watch TV, I won't be back down for a while, so be responsible. Okay kids? Oh and Greg, try not to be too loud. I don't know if the neighbors have moved in yet but it's better to be on the safe side," he announced.

By then even more people had showed up and the music had gotten a lot louder. This no doubt was nowhere near the huge keg parties the popular kids probably had on a regular basis, but still it felt kinda good to be hanging out with a beer buzz in a room full of people swaying to a song I wasn't even sure I liked, followed by one I did, and then one of my favorites.

To my surprise strains of Ricky had begun to fill the room; it was the song *Other Days* from *Sunset on Sunset*. (Greg had evidently decided not to be predictable and play *Lanie, Lanie*, the album's most famous song.) Every once in a while a slight hiss or crackle would emit from the speakers, but for the most part Greg seemed to have a good copy of the record.

I made my way over to the corner where the record player was and tapped Greg on the shoulder. He didn't look very surprised to see me.

"Hey Steve, I figured you would make me play at least one Ricky and the Sleepers song, so I decided to beat you to the punch." he announced as he flipped through a pile of CDs stacked next to the stereo. Apparently one Ricky Stevenson song was all I was going to get.

"I didn't know you had *Sunset on Sunset* on vinyl. Would you be willing to sell it by any chance? I've been looking for a copy for ages. I'll give you a fair price for it."

"Sorry, Steve, but it's my dad's and he never sells his records."

"Oh well, it was worth a shot."

"Yeah, my dad's always been a pretty big Ricky fan, in fact he knew this guy in LA who had a copy of *Summer Ride* with the original cover."

"Are you serious?" I asked Greg. The original cover of *Summer Ride* was pulled because the record company didn't approve of the photo of the girl wearing a bikini. Emcee records claimed the photo was too risqué but many experts have since claimed the photo was pulled because she looked as if she might have been racially mixed. Whatever the reasons were, an original copy of *Summer Ride* could fetch thousands.

"Yeah this guy used to be in the music industry and he got it as a promo or something. I saw it once when we were at his house. The girl on the cover was pretty hot," Greg said.

...

Later that night I had somehow managed to lose Greg and the rest of my friends and I found myself in a corner talking to Jill Jensen. Jill had been best friends with Wendy Summers back in eighth grade but somewhere between then and now she had dyed her hair a deep red and turned into one of the Goth kids that hung out under the bleachers. I looked at her long black dress and overdone eye makeup and wondered if she was even wearing a costume, but of course, I didn't have the nerve to ask.

"So Steven," she was saying, "You need to tell me more about Greg. I mean he's into girls right?"

I hadn't been paying attention up until that point-instead letting the beer do its thing-but I heard that last sentence quite clearly and it jolted me back to reality.

"Wait, What? Why do you think that? No way, there is NO way I mean I know Greg, he likes Kelly Rand," I mumbled semi-coherently.

"Damn Steven, just how many beers have you been drinking?" she asked while giving me a direct stare that went through to my bones.

"I was just wondering is all," she continued. "Greg has all this goofy furniture and that crazy bike and he is kind of obsessed with vintage stuff. Oh, and I'm not saying he's vain or anything but Greg seems to really be into looking a certain way. Not like most guys. Anyway I don't care if he is I don't believe in judging people, I'm just curious is all."

"I care about how I look, and I like vintage clothes, and old records. Oh my God, you could have just been describing me. Is that what people at this school think of me? You don't think I'm--you know, that way--do you?" I gulped. Oh God what if people think I am. "I don't care if other people are. I don't, I swear, but I like girls. I love girls."

"Everyone knows you like girls, Steve, we all remember how you used to lust after Veronica Whatshername in sixth grade, da-amn are you paranoid," she responded.

Veronica Winchell was the prettiest girl in sixth grade. She wasn't my first crush, just the first one I ever had the nerve to act upon. I had been a transparent fool, chasing after her, and always picking her first for my team in gym. I had spent half the year passing notes among my friends and continually pestering her friends about what Veronica thought of me. Finally she relented and let me take her to see a movie about a boy who switched bodies with his father.

I tried to follow Dave's advice and put my arm around her, but Veronica brushed it off, saying she was trying to watch the movie. The date perked up a little bit after the movie ended and she even let me kiss her as we waited by the pay-phone for her mom to pick us up. It had been the first kiss for both of us--but it must not have done as much for her as it did for me because two weeks later she had officially become "the girlfriend" of Jerrod Arden.

I never quite got what Jerrod had that I didn't. It must have been his skee ball prowess. It seemed like every time my friends and I went to the Crazy Castle to play miniature golf we saw the two of them in the arcade portion of the castle holding a wad of tickets giggling as they decided what prize to share. Nothing shouted sixth grade love trinket like a lime green plastic kazoo. Unfortunately for Jarrod, Veronica's father got transferred and her family moved to Wisconsin the next fall.

Surely I had not been as transparent about Justine. Sixth grade was a long time ago; I had matured a lot since then hadn't I? Oh why had I told Greg I liked her? Why had I told anyone? The popular people where probably laughing at me behind my back and taking bets on when I would finally get up the nerve to ask Justine out. I imagined a phony date where she would stand me up on purpose while the rest of her friends watched from across the street and laughed and laughed...

"Steve, Steve, Steven, hello earth to Steven," a voice quickly snapped me out of my temporary reverie. "Huh what," I mumbled, just before I remembered where I was.

Jill was still there and she was asking about Greg. She thought Greg was gay or something but I wasn't clear why she cared. Maybe Jill liked Greg and thought he didn't like her back so she assumed he must not be into girls or something. Man, Jill and Greg; that would be the strangest couple ever.

"I think Greg is into vintage clothes and stuff because his grandma owns this antique store and he told me his mom owns a vintage clothes store in L.A., you know and... Oh my God, who is that? ..."

My voice trailed off because I had glanced behind me and saw Greg involved in a liplock with someone. The back of her head looked familiar but I couldn't quite place her.

Jill saw the kiss at the same time as me and groaned.

"God, I should have guessed. I hope suddenly this party isn't overrun by Dan Parker and all his lemmings. If that happens I am so out of here." She rolled her eyes and continued "Why do guys always like that annoying Kelly Rand anyway?"

Kelly Rand? Kelly was here--without the popularity posse? Duh--that's who Greg was kissing. I thought the back of that head looked familiar, and no wonder. I sat behind Kelly in English every day. I started to say something to Jill but suddenly my world stopped as I was interrupted by her lips. Now we were the ones involved in an intense makeout session.

Was Jill using me to make a point to Greg? Did Greg even know she liked him, or was she just as drunk as me? What the hell time was it anyway? All of these questions would have to be answered later for the moment I was busy contemplating if tonight would finally be the night all high school males dream of.

After all, weren't countless television shows, movies and news reports constantly telling us one thing? Every teenage male in America but you is getting some (with the possible exception of Stuart Meeley). The popular kids are having orgies every night while you listen to records by a guy who drove into a river. Who besides you even still has a record player anyway? Forget Ricky Stevenson; concentrate on the present, for this is what life is truly about.

Jill released her lips for a few moments and looked at me in disbelief. It was a look that said; is that *Steve White*? Oh

God not *Steve White*! Did anyone see us? Just how drunk was I? Or maybe it was just a look of momentary confusion.

Jill looked down at her watch and yelled "Shit! Oh God I was supposed to be home two hours ago! Shit shit shit!"

Then she ran up the stairs--yelling: "Mr. Lewis, Mr. Lewis can you take me home?"

Meanwhile, I sat down against the wall ignoring the blackish gothgirl lipstick smeared on my shirt and watched the glitter from my Michael Jackson Jacket fall off in droves onto the new carpet as the world began to spin.

Chapter 15
The Day of the Dread

"Did you have fun last night Steve?" a voice from the heavens boomed above me. I opened my eyes and saw two dark figures partially blocking the blinding light but sadly doing nothing to ease the accompanying nightmarish headache. I blinked several times and after a few seconds the dark blobs morphed themselves into people.

"Rough night?" Greg was perched over me, and worse his father was perched alongside. Oh God, I would probably never be invited over here again.

"You've never been drunk before have you?" Greg asked.

"Of course I ha-" I stopped mid-sentence due to the fact that Mr. Lewis was still right there.

"It's okay Steven. I know what goes on in high school, and I knew there would probably be some drinking, but everyone got home safely and your friend Jill is okay in case you are wondering." He handed me some aspirin and water then continued. "I would much rather have a party where a few people drink, but I know what is going on, than be one of those parents who never lets their kids touch the stuff then as soon as I am out of town they throw a huge out of control party."

Mr. Lewis was talking about me and he didn't even know it. Last year I had thrown a huge party under those very circumstances. I thought it would get me in with the popular crowd. It had but only for that night. By the time Monday rolled around they had forgotten who I was. I had also blown most of my money on beer and was grounded for a month and a half due to my father's discovery of a large pile of cans and plastic cups behind space 128. I had thought I had gotten them all, but as usual I thought wrong. Jeanne of course was quick to rat me out. I don't know how she heard about it since she had spent the night at her best friend's across town. It had been the only wild party I had ever really been to, and the only previous time I had ever been genuinely drunk.

"Last night I called your house and told your mother you fell asleep while watching a movie and asked if it was okay for you to stay here tonight. She said it was alright, just don't go home looking like that--no offense," Greg said.

I glanced at my jacket which was now missing most of its glitter and the T-shirt I had put on under it now reeked of beer. The smell of the shirt made me gag, but somehow I made it to the bathroom before I threw up. I took off the jacket and tried to ignore the odor of the shirt as I gingerly made my way toward the kitchen. Greg was there holding some of his old clothes.

"Take a shower, and put these on, then join us for breakfast. You should probably eat something," he said.

...

At Greg's breakfast table I shifted my food around with the fork trying to avoid any more potentially gag inducing fumes, while trying to avoid eye contact as much as possible. Unfortunately Mr. Lewis had caught on rapidly and my eyes landed directly on his.

"I am so sorry Mr. Lewis," I mean I hardly ever drink; I guess I don't have much of a tolerance built up. I promise you I will vacuum up the glitter and fix or pay for any damage," I told him as guilt seeped through my every word.

Mr. Lewis gave an exasperated sigh and said,

"You are just a young man who has done what millions of people have done before, believe it or not you are not the first person to get drunk and make out with someone. You are a good kid I can tell, not like some of those kids Gregory knew in Monroeville. They would have drunk all my beer, drove over my lawn with their trucks, and then expected me to clean the dirt from their fenders. Now drink some water Steven, and you should probably call your mother. Greg says she didn't sound angry when he called last night."

I took a large gulp of the ice water, until that moment water had never been so refreshing in all my life. I was starting to feel a bit better, but then I thought of what most certainly lay ahead.

"It's not my mother I am worried about," I told Mr. Lewis.

"Maybe your father will understand too, he's got quite a past far as I can tell," he said.

"No he wouldn't understand at all, trust me. My Dad doesn't have a past. In fact I am pretty sure he's the most boring person in the world," I mumbled.

"It's always the boring people who have the pasts," Mr. Lewis' responded.

...

It turned out I didn't need to worry about my father after all since a note on our bulletin board said that he and Jeanne had gone to buy supplies for her science fair project. I just wanted to go up and crawl into bed for the rest of the day, but I couldn't risk avoiding my mother.

She was in the kitchen getting ready to bake those biscuits that come in a long cardboard tube. (Why did everyone have to cook when the thought of food made my internal organs act like they were preparing for the Olympic gymnastics team anyway?)

"How was your party Steven?" Mom asked, looking up from the cookie sheet.

"It was okay," I replied. "We watched a bunch of movies but I guess I fell asleep during *Nightmare on Elm Street,*" I said.

"Ugh how anyone can watch, let alone sleep during one of those awful gory movies is beyond me, but I guess it was Halloween," She replied.

"You guys aren't mad are you? I was too tired to come home, in fact I'm still pretty tired." I said yawning for effect.

"Of course not, we wouldn't want you to drive when you are too tired," she said and looked up towards me. "By the way where are your clothes? I am doing a load of laundry later."

"Oh I left them at Greg's, I'll get them Monday. I spilled coke on the front of my shirt plus I would have felt stupid driving through town in the Michael Jackson outfit the day after Halloween, you know," I said. "Do you mind if I go upstairs now?"

She nodded and I headed toward my room, after making a quick pit-stop at the car to retrieve the garbage bag full of my beer stained salute to the gloved one. I threw the bag under the bed promising myself I would wash Monday while she was at work--and soon fell into a deep sleep awakened only by voices offering me biscuits which I sleepily declined.

Chapter 16
The Thrift Store Score

I didn't see Jill at school Monday which was a relief since I wasn't in the mood for the awkward moments that were sure to follow. My hopes that my friends, acquaintances, and anyone else who knew my name had either gone home or been in another room during my drunken make-out session were dashed once I joined our table at lunch. My friends couldn't stop talking about the party.

"Ah, here comes the man of the hour," Stuart announced as I walked up "We hear you got a little hot Goth girl action last Friday."

I don't know where Stuart got off gossiping about me when according to half the school he had stood up on a table in the backyard and sang along off key to a Sinatra song. What Greg was doing playing Sinatra at a high school party anyway is beyond me, he was probably raiding his father's record cabinet and living out his rat pack fantasies in an effort to woo Kelly Rand. Evidently it worked. I guess it's too bad I look like Ricky Stevenson and not Ol' Blue Eyes. Oh well.

I ignored the accompanying snickers of my friends and looked around the cafeteria. As usual most of the other clusters of students were completely ignoring us. Maybe the party hadn't garnered as much attention as I suspected.

"I would totally do a Goth girl. I have always been a sucker for the whole dark woman of mystery vibe myself, and you two make a cute couple: the dead rock and roller and the woman who wants to be a zombie," Joey said, as usual trying to garner a laugh via the embarrassment of others.

Since I had not heard any stories of Joey making out with anyone lately or ever for that matter, I found it easy to come up with a sensitive comeback.

"Sorry you didn't have much fun as me at the party, maybe next time you will remember to bring your blow up doll."

"We were all pretty drunk. I bet Steve doesn't even remember kissing Jill," Dave came to my defense.

"Oh I remember alright. How could you not? Trust me Jill is a great kisser. You guys need to remember one thing, she went after me. She saw what she wanted and she went after it. I admire that in a woman. In fact if Jill didn't have to get home I might just be telling you guys about something a little bit more than just her lips if you know what I mean. Now if you don't mind, I am out of fruit punch," I said, then got up and walked towards the locker room where the vending machine was located. I felt relieved to get away.

...

After school I headed to bike racks as usual wishing my father paid enough for me to purchase some sort of car. I was thinking of reporting him to the people in charge of child labor laws when I heard an asthmatic gasp behind me. Ronald Meeley, Stuart's clone-like little brother was standing there catching his breath.

"I'm glad I found you," he gasped. "I was just over at Highland Thrift looking for old comic books when I saw that record by that guy you like."

I stood dumbfounded for a few minutes trying to picture twelve year old Ronald shopping at thrift stores.

Maybe he was trying to shake off the Meeley genes in order to become a hipster in training. Or maybe he just really liked comic books. Oh well, who cared anyway, what did he just say?

"Wait, What record?" I asked him.

"I dunno, just some record by that guy everyone says you look like."

"Why didn't you buy it for me? I would pay you back double," I said.

"I didn't have any money, but if you see any really old comics buy them for me and I will pay you double," he responded.

"Oh okay sure, I gotta go" I answered then hopped on my bike and flew through town.

···

As I got to the thrift store a college student was just leaving, his arms overflowing with records. I did a quick prayer; *God please please don't have him have taken my Ricky Stevenson albums*. I was hoping that the Lord would respond despite my family's somewhat spotty church attendance records. Perhaps somewhere up there God understood that Sunday was a truly sacred day when people rented a lot of storage spaces.

Once inside Highland, I noticed a new looking grey Rubbermaid bin beneath the old familiar stacks of records, and rushed to it first. This was undoubtedly what Ronald had been talking about. Inside were piles of the type of records you almost never see at thrift stores, someone must have donated their entire collection. Why on earth anyone would do this in a city with three used record stores was completely beyond me, but I have always been the type to thrive off of the stupidity of others. I quickly checked my wallet--a twenty--thank you lord!

Come on Ricky. Oh please, oh please, still be in here, I muttered under my breath. It was part wish, and part desperate plea, but mostly a prayer to a God I tend to ignore when not convenient.

Ricky was there in the form of a worn copy of *Sunset on Sunset*. I quickly snatched it up. Finally I held in my hands the famous cover photo of Ricky driving his '59 Corvette down Sunset Blvd, with the wind blowing his dark brown hair everywhere and the sun melting into the shimmering Pacific Ocean in the background. A quick look inside revealed that yes the record itself was inside and not too scratched. You wouldn't think that *Sunset on Sunset* would be so hard to find. Thousands of copies were pressed, but it's usually hard to find because people never give their copy away or sell it to a used record store.

Every time one of the local music shops gets their hands on a copy of *Sunset on Sunset* they charge at least fifty dollars for it. Not being the type of person who usually has fifty bucks on my person at one time, I would have to go back home only to discover I had just spent the last of my money on something stupid and non-returnable. Since I wouldn't have enough until my next payday, I would humbly ask Dad for an emergency paycheck advance.

Not only would Dad turn me down every time, but he would also torture me with his standard financial responsibility lecture for good measure. I had heard that particular speech approximately three hundred times before. In fact I had memorized it by the time I reached third grade. So by the time I actually managed to scrape up the fifty dollars, the record itself would be long gone.

The grey bin also contained a copy of *Drive Into The Sky* which I grabbed even though I already had two. I also bought three Beatles albums (none rare, dammit), some Van Morrison, and some 80's stuff for Jeanne. The grand total of my purchases: $8.75. Sometimes I just adore the wasteful nature of this land of the free.

On my way out I almost knocked over Jill Jensen. "Steve I just want to apologize for..." she began, but since I was still in my euphoric state, I interrupted her.

"Oh yeah, yeah—it's okay, Look if you are into records at all you have to go check the grey bin. It has good stuff, trust me. This will be your only chance before the vultures swoop in"

Jill looked at me questioningly and asked

"The vultures?"

"Yeah, you know, all the record collectors, the used record store owners, the college students, a good selection will not last"

"Doesn't that make you a vulture?"

"Oh yeah I am totally a vulture and for once I found a fresh kill early. I just got *Sunset on Sunset*. I have been looking for this on vinyl for years. You have to come listen to it. Come on, I live really close by."

We must have made an odd sight. Jill walking along in yet another long black dress with me beside her desperately trying to hold a pile of records and walk a bike at the same time. Why, oh why, hadn't I opted for one of those old fashioned baskets that goes above the front tire. Forget style, I could have really gone for some utilitarian convenience right then. The records were slipping everywhere and didn't come close to fitting inside my backpack. Jill offered to carry some, but I brushed her off with what I hoped was a somewhat masculine display of nonchalance by casually saying.

"Nah I got it, thanks."

When we finally got to the house I waved to Mom, did a quick intro of Jill, and we proceeded upstairs to my room. It wasn't until the last song began that I began to realize the absurdity of the situation. Here I was playing songs that were thirty some odd years old for a girl whose own musical tastes no doubt filed thrash metal under the category of easy listening. Like me, Jill was a lifer in the Chalmers County School District. We had been in various classes since kindergarten, yet somehow, I had missed her transition from the girl with the pigtails and the *Strawberry Shortcake* lunchbox to full blown vampire queen.

It was as if Jill woke up one day, burned all her normal clothes, walked into an occult bookstore, or mortuary in her pajamas and said, "Transform me, I am short of cash but I do have two pints of blood here in my backpack. What sort of look can I get in exchange?"

After the song ended, Jill looked at me and said

"That was pretty good."

"What?" I responded.

"I said that was pretty good, I am not normally that much into oldies, but that wasn't bad. He's a pretty good guitar player. I don't always listen to Goth music and hard core you know. Most people take one look, and I can tell they have already judged me. Like, oh my God she is wearing black lipstick. Oh no! Watch the cat before she tries to sacrifice it to the devil. I mean I am not even that much into the whole Goth scene anymore." Jill paused a minute to spit out her gum.

"My ex-boyfriend Jesse got me into the bands and the whole underground scene but now it's just boring and the music is all the same. I mean how many more times am I going to end up at some concert listening to yet another band with the words *testament* or *sacrifice* somewhere in the title?" She said, rolling her eyes.

I ignored the eye roll, which was a Jill Jensen trademark. I figured you had to have a certain amount of disdain for the public at large if you were going to carry around a black lunchbox, featuring a pattern of burning skulls, as a purse. What I couldn't tell was whether or not she considered me a part of this public that was so beneath her.

"I totally know what you are saying," I told Jill, even though I really didn't.

"I mean just because I like Ricky Stevenson doesn't mean I think I am him or something. I like all kinds of music-well except for most country and all rap, but hey I don't count rap as music anyway."

"Oh God, me neither," she said and glanced down at her watch.

"Look Steve I gotta go, but before I do I just want to say one thing. I was going to apologize to you for the other night, but I changed my mind. I'm not sorry for kissing you. You're a really good kisser, anyway see you around, bye."

I had been hoping for a goodbye kiss but since Jill stood up so abruptly I figured it wasn't going to happen. Oh well, from my experience good bye kisses usually didn't involve that much passion anyway. They were usually more of a quick peck.

...

After Jill had left I bounded downstairs whistling *Lanie, Lanie* the last track on *Sunset on Sunset,* Part of its chorus going through my brain.

> *Oh Lanie Lanie,*
> *You're my sweet Elaine.*
> *When you're around*
> *You stop all of my pain*
> *I forget all my troubles,*
> *I can't feel the rain*
> *Oh Lanie Lanie...*

As I reached the bottom of the stairwell, I nearly ran over Mom, who was carrying a fresh batch of laundered clothes up to her room.

Despite the fact that she is the one who works outside the home, Mom is the one who does the majority of our laundry. This is because she is convinced that Jeanne, Dad, or I will ruin every piece of the family's clothing should we try to figure out the complex machinery that makes up the set of harvest gold Kenmores sitting in the basement.

Although she is worried that we might shrink everything or create bleach stains, I think Mom's most pressing concern is that we will forget to empty out Dad's pockets before we do a load. My father's pockets are always filled to brim with nuts, bolts, scraps of paper, rubber bands, sticks of gum, hard candies, and of course the omnipresent black markers he uses to constantly label things. He is forever picking up loose odds and ends from our place, putting them in his pockets, and forgetting them. You can tell Mom has recently done laundry when you see little piles of these items stacked atop the washer or dryer. Should she forget to empty the pockets our clothes would soon be covered in an amalgamation of gum, rust stains and black marker ink.

I figured out how to use the washer myself one day when I ran out of clean underwear while Mom was at work, and it was about to come in handy for washing my stained Halloween costume, but my laundering prowess was a skill I had decided not to share with Mom and Dad. After all I have enough chores as it is.

"You certainly seem in a good mood, is it because of that girl who was just here?" Mom asked, upon hearing my off key whistle.

"Oh she's just a friend, I know she dresses kinda crazy but she is a really good person at heart," I responded. "Anyway I just invited her to listen to my newest find; I finally got *Sunset on Sunset* on vinyl. I've been looking for it for ages."

"I remember having a copy of that when I was your age," Mom said. "Let me guess, it's valuable now, I should have held on to mine."

"Well it's not worth thousands or anything," I said. "It's just harder to find than some of their other albums. Anyway who cares, I'm never going to sell mine anyway."

"Well congratulations on your find, just don't tell your father. I will never quite understand why the man never learned to appreciate the music of Ricky Stevenson." She said giving me an odd smile.

"Oh me neither," I said.

Chapter 17
The Key

Every November the National Association of Storage Professionals or NASP, holds their annual convention in Cincinnati, Ohio. Owners of storage facilities from all over the country come and listen to exciting lectures on topics like: *Preventing Water Damage:* twenty tips to protect your facility, or *Insurance:* how much do you really need? There are also booths featuring door and lock manufacturers, storage franchisers, alarm specialists, and more. I know this because when we were younger, my parents would go every year and drag Jeanne and me with them. While we would swim in the hotel's heated indoor pool and wander around the waterfront with one of our parents the other would return from the convention loaded up with brochures and various free Frisbees or sun-visors that said things like *Academy Locks:* featuring the new 3000 series.

As we got older, Mom and Dad would go to the convention together leaving Jeanne and I to our own devices. We discovered that the portion of Cincinnati in which we stayed actually gave Delacourte a run for its money on being the most boring place on earth. We ended up spending most of the time watching whatever bad movies happened to be playing at the nearby movie theater or wandering the hotel gift shop staring at the plastic snowglobes and having contests to see who could come up with the tackiest item the place sold that year.

Finally last year my parents let Jeanne stay at her best friend's, and put me in charge of the Stor'N'More while they went to the convention together. I guess when you are over fifty years old nothing shouts romantic weekend like wandering around a convention hall looking at booths that showcase cardboard boxes. Unfortunately, last year I dissolved my father's trust by holding the keg party. This year he has said that other than going to school I will not be able to set foot outside the house for a year if I so much as invite one friend over. Dad has paid Jeanne off to be his spy and, as I know from experience, there is nothing she loves to do more than narc on her big brother. I could already tell it was going to be one boring weekend.

...

Although I am only seventeen years old, I am completely able to take care of all aspects of running the Stor'N'More. This is a good thing because after Mom and Dad left for the convention the only other person around was Jeanne and she is completely useless. By the time I had turned fifteen I had become an official part time employee, but Jeanne had managed to weasel her way out of having to hold any actual responsibility. She did this by refusing to learn how to handle the office affairs of the Stor'N'More.

Now I would never have had the guts to pretend I had no idea what was going on after my father had spent an entire day showing me the forms and telling me what to do, but Jeanne did exactly that. What was even worse was the fact that Dad had completely fallen for her act, saying:

"Well the whole rental process is pretty complicated and there are an awful lot of forms. How about we go over them another time? I am sure you will get it then okay?"

He honestly seemed to believe that Jeanne couldn't figure out why we needed contracts and liability release forms, and which was which, and that people need to sign by the X not wherever they damn well pleased. It was as if he had been struck by a bout of temporary amnesia. Believe me Jeanne knows which form is which, she just happens to be one of those people who "accidently" drop one of the dishes they are washing so that they will never be asked to wash dishes again.

My sister has been on every single honor roll list since kindergarten. While I struggle with trinomials, French grammar, and the intimate details of the Revolutionary War she breezes through gifted and advanced placement classes with no problem. You would think Jeanne the genius had been switched at birth, but since she has the same dark brown hair and dark blue eyes of my father along with the pert nose and bad eyesight of my mother I know this is not the case.

Jeanne has no need to be an employee of the Stor'N'More. Most of the time she makes do with her allowance and gets extra money from extra chores and after school tutoring. Whenever she gets low on these funds, Jeanne hangs around until Dad recruits her to help load and unload one of the spaces or sweep up the office, then he pays her in cash. Having the distasteful title of storage facility employee would crimp Jeanne's style. What would the college interviewer from Harvard say?

That Saturday morning I came downstairs only to find Jeanne sitting in my spot in front of the den TV watching *Saved by the Bell*. I loathe that show. I also hate any weekend morning where I cannot sleep in because of the remote possibility that someone may actually want to rent a space in November.

"I need this TV," I told Jeanne while I stood directly in front of it.

"No you don't--you can go upstairs and watch your own TV or Mom and Dad's," She muttered, in between bites of her Cheerios.

"You know I need to be able to hear the bell in case anybody comes to the office--or do you want office duty?" I glared at her with my arms crossed.

Jeanne glared at me in return for a few seconds then said

"Dad doesn't allow me to work in the office."

"Well I am in charge this weekend, and I think you could handle it," I told her.

"Nobody ever comes here this late in the year you know that--now move." she said.

I started to respond but to our amazement, the intercom's bell rang out with its shrill ding.

"You wanted to sit here--I guess you have office duty," I told Jeanne, but she just grumbled, "you can have the TV," and fled upstairs.

...

A short balding man was at the counter when I entered the office. He didn't look very happy to be here.

"I'm trying to clear out number 116, my father's locker--it's a real mess. Do you have boxes?" He asked.

"We sell both cardboard boxes and plastic bins that will keep your items better protected from the elements. You can select from those on the wall over there we have them all in stock except for the large cardboard," I said pointing at the wall where we sell a variety of boxes, locks, and tools all at a deliberately higher price than you can get at the local hardware store. (My father had sold the last of the large cardboard ones to Mrs. Rand for her Christmas party.)

He eyed the large cardboard box display, as if he hadn't just been told that we were out. "Can I buy that one?" He asked.

"That's actually just a display--but we have a comparable size in plastic," I told him.

"I just need to move it to my apartment, a few blocks away. Why can't I buy that box right there? When you get more in you can make a new display," he said irritably.

Great, a pain in the neck. Hey you--I could be sleeping right now--but whatever.

"Sure I can sell it to you, but it has been on display for quite some time so I am just warning you, it's gonna be dusty," I said.

"That's fine, I don't care," was his response.

"Okay then just let me get the stepladder."

As I grabbed the box of the top of the shelf I nearly gagged on the dust. Ugh. Didn't we ever clean up here? The dust had now formed a square outline from where the box had been. In the middle of the square was something metal catching the reflection of the lights overhead but I couldn't quite tell what it was.

I quickly sold Mr. Picky the dusty box at a discount and five of our medium size ones, then I scrawled a note to my father that number 116 had decided not to renew his contract--perhaps a follow up phone call was in order? I watched out the window as he slowly dragged the boxes toward his space then grabbed the feather duster from beneath the counter.

The lump beneath the box turned out to be a key. It was one of the old style ones so it was undoubtedly useless by now but still I found myself trying to pry it up. Only a corner of the key had caught the reflection, the rest of it was all rusted and had somehow congealed itself to the metal top of the shelf. I climbed down again and grabbed some rags, a screwdriver, and some 409. After letting it sit in the 409 for a few minutes, I managed to wedge the key up with the screwdriver and get it loose. I wiped it down with the rags and took a closer look, I could just barely make out the number seventeen.

So we did have a key to seventeen after all. I set it into the key machine and made myself a new copy. Tonight if no one was around I was going to see if I could get number seventeen's door to open. Another space may just bring in more money to this operation, especially since seventeen is one of the largest lockers in our complex.

...

Space 116 didn't get cleared out until later that afternoon, when the customer finally drove off with a rented U-Haul packed to the gills. I did a quick walk around of all the lockers, or spaces as Dad insists I must always call them, saying:

"A locker Steven, is where you keep your schoolbooks. These are storage spaces, they are larger and much more versatile than any locker."

I usually just ignore my father, he reads too many of those regulation binders the Stor'N'More headquarters is always sending us. As far as I am concerned any place where you put stuff inside, shut a door, lock it up and forget about it constitutes a locker.

Shortly after the gate closed and the U-Haul had pulled out onto Highland, I did a quick check around the place making sure no one was about, then headed over to seventeen. As usual the dent really didn't look that bad to me, sure it was large but it didn't really look like it would cause the door to not open at all. I put the new key in, and slowly turned it. It seemed to work making the telltale click that new or old our doors' locks always do. The door lifted smoothly and easily just as I thought it would. There seemed to be no problem from the dent whatsoever. Since the largest lockers were usually equipped with fluorescent overhead lights I reached for the switch just in case they still worked, much to my amazement they did. Then I let out the largest gasp of my life.

Chapter 18
Inside Locker Seventeen

"Holy Shit!"

The words behind me caused me to jump about three feet in the air. As I looked behind me I saw Jeanne standing with the same opened mouth look of awe I had just had a second earlier.

"Is this all real?" she asked.

"I-I don't know lets go in and see," I said.

"Does the door work?" She asked me. "I mean we won't get locked in will we?"

"You stay out here and I will go in and check." I said stepping inside. I rolled the door down and back up a few times then announced:

"It seems to work just fine."

Jeanne seemed a little unsure but she joined me within the realm of this new found wonderland and I rolled the door back down most of the way so no one else would see the contents within.

Despite the fact that I had spent my entire life believing that seventeen had not been opened since the mid 1970's, It appeared that had not been the case at all. The space was almost completely dust free and the inside had been fitted with the newest innovations for storage facilities found within the pages of *Storage Monthly* magazine. (A really thrilling read.) It had a reinforced fireproofed wall system and a new looking ceiling that had sprinklers installed. The floor had been covered with the same type and pattern of vinyl flooring that my father had put in our kitchen three years ago. Unlike any of our other storage spaces, seventeen was fully wired, several electrical outlets lined the walls, and there was a thermostat in the corner.

Though our largest spaces can easily fit a car, I had never seen anyone store one inside them--until now. It wasn't just any car, but a turquoise blue and white Corvette. I have never been one of those guys who could tell the exact date of a car just by looking at it, but I had the distinct impression that the one in front of me was a '59. I looked downwards and slowly read the numbers imprinted on the license plate while thinking there is no possible way, it cannot possibly be the real one. The plate in front of me was an old style black and yellow California license plate from the days long before personalized plates became all the rage. The numbers imprinted on it read CLJ 412, an exact match of the number I have memorized by heart due to repeated viewings of *The Greatest Hoax in Rock and Roll History*, which I have on videotape.

"Do you think this is the real one?" Jeanne asked me quietly.

"Well the fake one is at this car museum in Houston, and the ones they made for the movie and auctioned off were bought by people in LA--but God--I wish I knew the real VIN number of Ricky's car, just to be sure," I told her.

"How come you don't know that number? I thought you knew everything about Ricky Stevenson. Anyway what exactly is a VIN number anyhow?" Jeanne whispered. We both felt the need to speak in hushed tones, since we were in such an amazing and apparently forbidden place.

"V-I-N stands for Vehicle Identification Number-it's this number they put on every car kind of like a serial number. That's how they knew that one in Minnesota was a fake. The numbers didn't match. Anyway they never released the real number to the public, but this has got to be the real one I mean judging by everything else in here." I whispered back.

Besides the car, the storage space looked like a museum dedicated to Ricky Stevenson. Five gold records lined the walls, as well as framed copies of each of Ricky and the Sleepers albums. *Summer Ride* was framed twice with its first and second covers represented here. On closer inspection I noticed that each of the framed albums had signatures from all four band members including Ricky.

In the corner was a guitar case. I walked over and opened it up revealing an old Les Paul with a sunburst finish. It had to be *the* guitar, Ricky's 1958 custom Les Paul with a sunburst finish named Lu Lu Mae. There was an amplifier alongside but I didn't dare plug her in. Instead I stood for a few moments quietly strumming the world's most famous guitar, and trying to get over my shock.

All around the sides of the space were stacks of plastic bins of the exact same type I had tried to sell the customer who rented 116 this morning. Jeanne opened one, and it revealed a collection of magazines dating from the 1950's, to the tabloid that had come out last month announcing *Ricky Stevenson murdered-bones found in Tallahassee backyard!* I left Jeanne to sift through the magazines and made my way over to the car.

After determining it to be alarm free, I reached into the Corvette's glove compartment. Inside was the registration, alongside a set of keys and a California driver's license belonging to a Richard M. Stevenson with the expiration dated August, 1966.

"I can't believe this," I said fingering the sacred license. "I mean Dad must rent this out to the actual Ricky Stevenson. He probably lives around here."

Jeanne looked at me oddly before she said "You really don't know do you?--even though it's so obvious."

"Don't know what?" I asked.

"Dad doesn't rent this space to Ricky Stevenson. Dad is Ricky Stevenson."

I couldn't help but laugh. That had to be the most preposterous thing I had ever heard.

"Come on Jeanne," I said. "Have you ever looked at Dad? He doesn't look anything like Ricky Stevenson. I'm so sure, Ricky Stevenson with graying hair and a beer gut straining his bad back all day moving around other peoples shit all day long. Yeah right, just call me Steven Stevenson."

"They have the same birthday," she said, still trying to convince me.

This was true. Ricky and my father did share a birthday a fact that I always thought was so cool, yet so completely wasted on Dad. I mean why couldn't I have been born on Ricky Stevenson's birthday? It was the one day when it was almost a guarantee that some cable channel would play a movie about Ricky's life, or a new documentary on his disappearance, and I had to spend it pretty much avoiding the TV altogether. Time I could spend watching: *The Ryman Auditorium celebrates the music of Ricky Stevenson* was instead spent listening to Dad grumble about getting older, and watching him unenthusiastically unwrap the same ratchet set he had received the previous year.

"Come on Jeanne," I said. "Just because someone shares a birthday with someone else doesn't instantly make them the same person besides it's not even the same year. Dad's a year younger than Ricky Stevenson."

"That's what he tells us. Look, it's been thirty years since he disappeared. If Ricky Stevenson is alive he is middle aged, and therefore looks like a middle aged man not a teenager anymore. He could be anybody, and if Ricky Stevenson is just some middle aged nobody living in a boring little town in Indiana, he would have learned how to blend in by now. In fact the only clue might be to look at his kids. Don't you think Ricky Stevenson would have a son who looks like Ricky Stevenson?"

"I still don't buy it," I told her. "Now come on let's see what's in the rest of these bins."

Chapter 19
Secrets in a Storage Space

The more we looked through the bins the more unlikely it seemed that this space could ever been rented by anyone except Ricky Stevenson or someone extremely close to him. Each bin contained stuff that would be mundane had it belonged to anyone else, but worth hundreds or possibly even thousands because of the magical name that was attached. We sifted through report cards, childhood drawings, photos, even one of those clay hand imprints you make in kindergarten. I found a set of yearbooks for Van Nuys High where Ricky had graduated in 1959 even though he was steadily rising up the charts.

One question constantly lingered in my mind. Who did all of this actually belong to? Was Jeanne right? Could Jack R. White, entrepreneur, father, and all around boring guy really be the reclusive Ricky Stevenson?

I didn't think for one second it could actually be Dad. For one thing everyone said Ricky was reclusive, and not really good with people yet my father had chosen a profession where he frequently came into contact with people he didn't know. Would someone who detested the public as much as Ricky Stevenson, really be at home behind the counter of a small business, making small talk, and convincing strangers that the Stor'N'More's deluxe package was really the only way to go? I don't think so.

I had also never heard my father really sing. Once in a while he would whistle or hum along with the radio but he never sang anything except for *Happy Birthday* and his rendition of that classic had gained no special notice from listening parties, and I had never heard Dad play any sort of instrument except for one time.

I had just bought my guitar, Lu Lu Belle, and was up in my room strumming and getting frustrated at my lack of learning to play quickly. In a typical Steven gesture, I was contemplating giving up on learning the guitar all together, like I had previously done with soccer, karate, and making a radio controlled airplane from a kit. Dad heard my awful strumming and the muffled curses accompanying my unsuccessful attempts at mastering the most basic chords, and decided to do an intervention before the guitar ended up being hurled from my second story window.

"Sounds pretty good Steven," He said while sitting on my bed.

"No it doesn't, it's too hard," I mumbled back.

"It takes time Steven, all things worth doing take time," he told me then picked the guitar up and did a blistering rendition of *Miserlou*.

"That was fantastic, play some more," I said.

"I'm afraid I can't," he told me. "That's the only song I know. It took me a long time to learn so I gave up. If I hadn't given up I think I could have become pretty good."

I had pretty much forgotten that moment up until now. Though I wouldn't consciously admit it, it was starting to seem possible that Dad might just be more than an average guy who knew one song on guitar. I quickly shook off these thoughts and glanced down at my watch. It was almost 10, Jeanne and I had spent hours in here and hadn't even realized it.

"Come on, we better go," I told Jeanne.

"Okay, just be sure to lock up. Do you really think it will all be here in the morning or is this some crazy dream we are both sharing?" She asked me.

"I don't know," I responded, then shut off the light and rolled down the door checking five or six times to make sure it was still locked.

...

When we got back to the house we were both jolted back to reality by the sound of the phone. I ran over to the counter and picked it up.

"Where the hell have you been Steven? We have called and called. Why can't I even trust you for five seconds?" It was Dad of course, thoughts that he may be the world's most famous missing person rapidly dissolving. He was your typical father and boy was he pissed.

"Answer me Steven. Where the hell have you two been?" Just in the backyard Dad. It seems that we have this car that may fetch millions at auction.

I tried to think as fast as I could, then I remembered that Jeanne had been pestering Mom all week about some movie she wanted to see.

"We went to see a movie, that dance one Jeanne wanted to see and we just got back. I was going to call but I thought it might be too late," I told him.

"You went to see that dancing movie? You had better not be trying to bribe your sister. I said no friends over, and I meant it. I've got my eye on you Steven, even though I am out of town I still have my eye on you, and don't you forget it," Dad was in full drill sergeant mode now.

"Yes sir, I won't have anyone over. I really am sorry, okay? Good night," I said after he finally let me hang up.

Why, oh why, couldn't I have remembered to bring the cordless? I wondered to myself before I headed off to bed.

Chapter 20
We Could Have Had It All

I didn't really sleep that night, who could under such circumstances? Instead I tossed and turned all night and let my imagination run wild. My mind's eye kept picturing news trucks from all over parked on every street in our little town, our little family their sole purpose for being here. Suddenly that weird kid in English class who wears all those vintage clothes would become the toast of the school.

Justine Weeks would be clamoring for my attention, while the rest of the popular kids would spend their days desperately trying to push past hundreds of entertainment show reporters in order to get near me. It would be the goal of every man woman and child in town to have their picture taken with me, or at least get their hands on an autograph from the former Steven J. White. I would of course now be known the world over as Ricky Stevenson Jr. Then we would move to Los Angeles or New York to a huge mansion that includes a bowling alley and a recording studio.

Or maybe my father was not Ricky Stevenson at all but had just been storing the car for a mysterious stranger. This stranger had willed all of the stuff to that nice family who was keeping his car in an Indiana Stor'N'More, and unbeknownst to us, had passed away several years ago.

After a night of tossing and turning I was awakened at 6:20. I don't think I had ever been awake that early before. Quietly I threw on my sweats and crept downstairs, only to find Jeanne at the breakfast table pouring copious amounts of sugar on her cereal.

"You didn't really sleep that good either," she said upon seeing me.

"Nope," was my response.

"Do you think it's really real or just some sort of a crazy dream we both had?" she asked.

"I'm pretty sure it's real," I said. "Let's go check."

The sun was rising as we headed outside giving everything a pinkish glow. In the distance we heard the freight train that passes behind our place every morning.

We slowly padded our way across the concrete squinting from the rising sun reflecting off the locker doors and shivering from the bitter cold. The new copy of the key was sitting on my dresser in the same place as I had put it the night before, a good indication that this situation could in fact be real. It still fit easily in the lock and the door rolled up once again revealing the car, the records and the boxes, same as before. I wondered if my horoscope that morning would read: Today your life will be irrevocably changed forever.

...

We spent the rest of the morning going through shifts, one of us would go through the bins inside, while the other one kept guard to make sure no one stopped by. Each box contained the same type of things we had seen the night before. There were personal items like old childhood mementos, as well as a great many items relating to Ricky's career as a rock and roll star. One of the bins contained posters from almost every concert Ricky and the Sleepers had ever performed, while several others were filled with newspaper and magazine chronicles printed during the height of Ricky's career. Not everything inside seventeen was from Ricky and the Sleepers heyday either. There were plenty of bins that contained various books, magazines, collectibles and other Sleepers ephemera that had come out after Ricky's disappearance. Whoever had regular access to locker seventeen stayed current with their collecting habits, and I came across an awful lot of the same newspaper and magazine articles I kept in my footlocker and on my haphazard bookshelf. In the bin that appeared to contain the most recent stuff I noticed a copy of this month's *Retrobeat* magazine featuring *Ricky Stevenson's Intimate Secrets: An old girlfriend tells all.* I hadn't even bought that one yet.

Jeanne and I had laid down a couple of ground rules for going through seventeen. During each of our shifts we pledged to go through only one box at a time, put everything within the box back in the exact order it originally was, and then put the box itself back in the exact spot where we had found it. After our shift was done we reported what we had seen to each other. By mid-afternoon it looked as if we had investigated every bin inside the space. I had started to worry that someone would need to visit their space or that Mom and Dad would arrive from the convention early when I heard the shrill wail of the camping whistle Jeanne was wearing around her neck.

I quickly stepped outside and rolled down the door all the way as I checked up and down the locker row. After I got it locked I banged my head on the soda machine my father had set near the lock, making a horrible racket.

"Are you okay?" Jeanne asked as she walked towards me.

"Oh yeah, fine. I heard the whistle is anyone here right now?" I asked

"A car pulled into the driveway but they were just turning around," she said.

"Oh okay, look since everything is pretty much back to where it was, I think we should go to lunch or something. I mean I need to get away from all of this for a while so I can try to figure things out."

"Sounds good to me, I am totally starved. I just need to take a shower first," she agreed.

After we had gotten ourselves cleaned up and I had checked seventeen several times to make sure it was secure we put the *Be back at...* sign up in the office door window and piled into mom's old Buick.

"I wish we could drive *it*," Jeanne said as she looked around the Buick's shabby green interior.

"Oh me too, but there is no way we can. Anyway the Corvette probably doesn't run. If you just let a car sit for years it stops working," I said.

"How could you just let a car that valuable just sit?" Jeanne asked.

"If whoever owns the Corvette tried to re-register it don't you think it would raise a few flags?"

"Dad owns it--you know he does. I think he should have switched license plates with the station wagon and drove it around the backroads at night. That's what I would have done," Jeanne said.

We ate lunch at Mandy's, a little sandwich place by the college. It was a very quiet meal with each of us not daring to talk. Jeanne and I had only one thing on our minds and we could not have it overheard. Finally as the waitress placed the check on the table I broke the silence by saying.

"Let's go for a walk."

Despite the fact that it was a rather chilly afternoon, Jeanne agreed, and we headed outside through the streets leading towards the university. As we passed huge houses with giant lawns, I kept thinking of our simple two-story house surrounded by a sea of concrete and storage lockers. Jeanne must have been thinking the same thing because she looked at me and said,

"We could have had all of this and more, I mean look at these huge lawns and the columns on that one. I always wanted to be one of the kids who lived in these houses. I remember when Jenny Atkins had her birthday party when I was seven. She got this swing-set for her huge yard, I was so jealous. I always thought if we would just move suddenly I would be popular like her, now it turns out all along we could have."

"I don't know. I am still not even sure it is him," I said. "I mean why would you choose to live at a storage place, if you had enough money to live anywhere in the world?"

"It's definitely Dad, no question," Jeanne responded. "Even if it isn't him there are so many questions that need to be answered. We have to confront him you know. The sooner the better as far as I'm concerned, but God it's going to be so weird."

We kept on walking until we hit the south end of the university. Just ahead of us lay the large outdoor amphitheater where Ricky Stevenson had played to a sellout crowd in 1961. We stopped in the middle of the grassy stage area, a place I had stood many times before.

"He played right here, in 1961, probably on this very spot," I told Jeanne.

"Yeah I know I have heard of that concert, come on I think we should go." she said unimpressed. "It's getting kind of cold and I think it may rain."

...

Mom and Dad didn't get home until pretty late that night so we didn't have a chance to talk. I guess it would all have to wait until tomorrow after school. Strangely enough I wasn't looking forward to the conversation. Maybe I wanted seventeen to be my secret, or maybe I was simply afraid of the truth. Would it be that Dad was just renting out the space, and I couldn't tell anyone or could *Dad* of all people be the elusive Ricky Stevenson himself?

Chapter 21
Idol Distractions

My whole life teachers have been labeling me distracted. Report cards, parent teacher conferences, and guidance counselors always seem to say the same things. There's the sugarcoated: Steven seems like a nice young man but he has trouble concentrating, the more direct: Steven is a daydreamer; he seems to need a little more direction, and of course the ever popular short and simple yet dreaded: Steven needs to pay attention more.

If you ask me it's all the fault of my teachers. If they put some effort into the educational process and actually made their classes interesting I wouldn't be so unable to concentrate in the first place. Now for once in my life I finally had a damn good excuse for my distracted nature and I couldn't tell anybody. Not a soul.

Everything pretty much clicked at breakfast. For the first time in my life I actually managed to wake up on time on a school day. In fact I was awake so early that I had time to eat breakfast at the table alongside my parents, two people who never quite grasped the concept of sleeping in.

"Good morning Steven, train wake you up?" Dad asked.

"Umm, yeah I guess," I responded.

"Yeah that damn train's become my alarm clock; anyway the house looks pretty good. I am going to trust that you didn't have people over this weekend," he said.

As I watched Dad saying these words, something clicked in my brain. Not only had I been hearing how much I look like Ricky Stevenson all my life but also that I look like my father, various relatives and friends would come to him and go:

"Jack--that boy of yours is looking more and more like his father every day."

I had never believed any of them before. I thought this was merely one of those lines people said when they couldn't think of anything else to say.

Then suddenly as I looked at Dad sitting there I began to picture him thirty years younger, with more hair on his head, and less lines in his face. I blinked a few times and there it was. My idol was sitting right in front of me, devouring a stack of store brand waffles. Those dark blue eyes that are just like mine (and like those of Ricky), his mouth, that nose, how could I have not noticed before--how could *anybody* not have noticed before? Dear God Jeanne was right; no doubt about it, my father was Ricky Stevenson.

"Steven what the heck are you staring at?" Dad grumbled at me. "Are you hiding something?"

Like *Ricky Stevenson* was the one to talk about hiding something.

"Steven--Steven, pay attention--you are going to be late to school," he continued before turning to my mother and asking.

"Why does that child always zone out like that?"

...

School went by in a flurry of "Steven White are you paying attention" speeches from my teachers and assorted comments from my friends like:

"Dude, Steven why are you spacing out? I bet you are thinking about Jill aren't you. She looks really hot now that she's not so Goth." Jill had recently started hanging out with Wendy Summers and her crowd again, and had shed her Gothic look in favor of an odd combination of punk, mod, and vintage. For some reason she kept her skull lunchbox purse.

My strategy of ignoring both my friends and my instructors and concentrating on my own thoughts worked pretty well until fifth period algebra class when I was snapped back to reality by Mr. Washington tapping on my shoulder and clearing his throat.

"Mr. White, although it may impress all of your friends that your busy social life allows you neither time for sleep, or quadratic equations, it does not impress me. Now as I have been saying for the past five minutes, you have an appointment with your guidance counselor."

Shit!, the appointment with Mr. Carmichael! I had completely forgotten about it. I ignored the laughs of my fellow classmates, packed up my stuff and walked down the hall toward the school office, all the while thinking--hey Carmichael I don't need any guidance right now seeing as how I just found out that I am the heir to a rock and roll fortune.

I sat down in the posture adjusting cheap plastic chair that had been designed by prisoners to demoralize all those who sat in them and glanced up at Mr. Carmichael, who was looking down at a file.

"Ah, Mr. White," he said, "nice of you to finally join me."

"Sorry, I forgot," I mumbled and looked down at my feet. Although normally I would do anything to get out of even two minutes of the overwhelming torture that is algebra, on this day I was in no mood to share my innermost hopes and dreams with a low level bureaucrat who had undoubtedly been forced to give his up long ago.

"So Steven, when I buzzed your algebra teacher, he told me that you are acting even more distracted than usual today. Is there any particular reason why?" he asked.

"No not really. I mean I didn't think I was. I guess I am just bored is all, my teachers need to make their classes more interesting you know," I sighed.

"Yes, so you have told me before. Tell me Steven, do you have any post-graduation plans? I know you are only a junior now, but it's coming fast."

I am thinking mansions and supermodels baby, Justine missed her chance--now it's time for Claudia Schiffer in a thong. "I'm thinking of going to Los Angeles, for college," I told him.

"Okay this is a start, it's the first time I have ever heard you mention something that sounds like it could be a plan. Do you have any particular colleges in mind?" Carmichael asked.

"I dunno--maybe UCLA or something," I mumbled. I am not sure why but guidance counselors always manage to bring out my most articulate side.

"Yes well I think this is good for a long term plan, but you should remember that UCLA is a very competitive school. Frankly Steve, your hmmm, shall we say distracted nature has made you mostly a C student."

(For the record, Mr. Carmichael got it wrong. I am not a C student. I am a B- student with occasional C+ tendencies. Anyway who cares--my father's secretly a millionaire--I don't need to worry about grades.)

"I think you should check out Dexter Community College," he continued. "Take a few classes, see if you like college life and find what interests you. You can get a lot of your general education classes out of the way for a lower price. Get yourself an A.A. Degree first then there will plenty of time to attend UCLA or another college in the L.A.

Area." Mr. Carmichael paused for a second and pulled a paper from a drawer.

"As long as we are on the subject, Dexter is having a preview night in a couple of weeks I really think it would be worth your while to go. Why don't you take this flyer." He said and handed me a fluorescent pink paper which I stuffed in my backpack as I stood up and muttered, "uh okay sound's good."

"Steven, sit down there are a couple more things I want to ask you," He said.

"Oh sorry, what?" I said as I slumped back into the evil posture chair.

"You do seem really distracted today. You are not having family problems are you?"

"No, nope my family's great." In fact my parents just got back from a fling at a tremendously romantic storage convention. They quite possibly renewed their vows in front of the packaging tape display.

"If you need to talk about anything, and I do mean anything at all feel free to tell me. It's what I am paid for Steven."

"No not really, I guess I am just tired or something," I said.

"Are you sure there is nothing bothering you Steven? I know how good it feels to get something off your chest. Come on give it a try."

"Look Mr. C., I am not being abused or tortured or anything like that. In fact it's not even about me at all." Oh crap a Freudian slip, dammit! I knew he was never gonna let me leave.

"Is it one of your friends? Some kind of girl trouble? I hear you and Jill Jensen are an item now."

What? How in the heck did he know that? What kind of a guidance counselor is this man anyway?

"No I just found out that somebody I know has this really big secret, and I can't tell anyone about it right now, okay."

"If it's one of your friends and they are in danger from someone or even themselves it's okay to tell me. You do know that, right Steven. You may even be saving their life."

For the love of God, I thought. What do spend your days memorizing after school specials or something? This is not a suicidal teen hotline, It's a damn guidance counseling session. All you are supposed to be doing is telling me how I have screwed up my chances to get into a decent school.

"No it's not anything like that. In fact this person is an adult and they don't know that I know their secret so I have to talk to them about it tonight. That's all."

"Are you sure it's not something you can tell me? I have signed an oath that I will keep personal matters between me and the student unless they put someone in physical danger."

Yeah right-by next week you will be on *Oprah* telling everyone how screwed up the son of Ricky Stevenson is.

"No it's not a big deal I just need to talk to them about it, and then everything will be fine."

"Oh alright, well I guess I will let you go as long as you promise to attend the Dexter preview night."

"Okay I promise. Dexter Community College preview night, I will definitely be there. See you later bye."

Chapter 22
The Family Meeting

When I got home from school I set my backpack at the kitchen table and noticed my mother at the counter rolling raw chicken around in a cornflake mixture. This could only mean one thing; we were having dinner as a family, an occasion that was becoming more and more rare. Usually I was over at a friend's, or Mom had to work late, or Jeanne was off somewhere. Dad however, was always around at dinnertime; especially if he thought there was a chance someone would make him some food.

I was relieved we were having a real dinner tonight. If Jeanne and I were going to confront Dad tonight I would much rather have a full stomach from some tasty cornflake chicken than from a frozen dinner.

"Steven you're home, good. Tonight your father wants to have a family meeting, you don't have any plans do you?" Mom said glancing up from the chicken.

"No, not really, am I in trouble or something? I didn't have friends over last weekend I swear," I said.

"No, no, it has nothing do with that there are just some things that we need to talk about," she said.

"Oh okay. Is Jeanne around?"

"I think she's watching TV. Why?"

"I just wanted to ask her something no big deal."

"Oh. Well I hope you two are getting along better."

"Yeah we are." It's amazing how solving the world's biggest mystery can really bond people together.

"Okay, well dinner should be ready in about an hour."

"How come we are eating so early?"

"Your father was hungry, He missed lunch I guess."

I left my mother to roll her chicken then ventured towards the den where Jeanne saw me and shut off the TV. She nodded her head towards the stairs, and we headed up to my room.

"I think he knows," she said plopping on my bed.

"Are you sure? I mean I left seventeen exactly the way it was before," I told her.

"He's been acting weird since I got home, and now we are having dinner really early so we can have a family meeting," she said.

"Yeah Mom told me, but Dad seemed normal this morning, so maybe it's nothing."

"Even if it is, we have to confront him tonight."

"Yeah, I guess you're right."

"Look Steven, I know I have never taken much of an interest before, but considering the circumstances I'd like to see some of your Ricky Stevenson stuff," Jeanne said as she wiped her glasses than examined the faded *Ricky Stevenson: Where is he Now?* poster that was over my bed.

From the looks of it we were the only two people that actually knew--well aside from our father that is.

"Sure I can show it to you. Just remember it's nothing like what's in seventeen," I told Jeanne.

"Duh I know that" she replied.

We spent the next hour going through my collection. It looked pretty meager considering what we had seen just two nights ago, but here it was. The only original sixties era Ricky Stevenson stuff I had been able to find over the years were a few of the record albums. I had three copies of *Drive into the Sky* as well as my prized find: *Sunset on Sunset*. I also had all of the old albums as CD reissues, and a copy of *Ricky! A Retrospective* and *Ricky Stevenson Rarities*.

Everything else was new stuff that had come out long after he had disappeared. There was the still mint-in-it's-package Ricky Stevenson doll Wendy Summers had gotten me for my birthday, the posters which lined the walls of my room, the notebook I had purchased in eighth grade, the magnets attached to my desk, The *Have You Seen Ricky?* pin attached to my backpack, the stickers affixed to my footlocker, and the corny Ricky Stevenson commemorative plate I had bought at the Salvation Army.

The bulk of my collection consisted of old newspapers and magazines with articles about Ricky, books about Ricky, and videotapes of practically every show or movie ever made about Ricky. Mom and Dad were never that happy about me having a TV and VCR in my room, but since I had bought both from Highland Thrift with money I made from work, they didn't have any right to complain.

"Who gets all the money from this stuff? I mean there have to be tons of royalties," Jeanne said as she flipped through a copy of *Guitar Riff Monthly* featuring an article about the songs of Ricky Stevenson.

"His dad was the only close relative that Ricky had at the time of the disappearance so he gets all of them. He eventually formed this giant profitable company called Ricky Stevenson Enterprises. He totally stole the idea from the Elvis Presley people. Even the name is totally unoriginal. Anyway he's now a multimillionaire. Check this out," I said and showed her the Ricky Stevenson Enterprises official souvenir stamp on the back of the commemorative plate.

"So I guess Ricky's dad is our grandfather. It's so weird to think that we actually do have some relatives on Dad's side. I mean what happens if people find out he's alive? Wasn't he declared dead?" she asked.

"I don't know if Ricky was ever officially declared dead because Bob Stevenson went on and on about how he was sure that his son was out there alive somewhere. He really milked the whole grieving father act. Every book on Ricky I have ever read says Ricky's dad ignored him and wasn't a good father at all and that they hated each other, but I guess Ricky didn't hate his dad as much as he claimed because he made him really rich," I said.

Our conversation was abruptly cut short by Mom's shouts of "Kids, Dinner!"

Before heading downstairs Jeanne and I gave each other one final look that said *oh my God, what have we gotten ourselves into?* Then we set forth towards the kitchen.

The first ten minutes of dinner were quiet as we were all busy consuming the chicken. I glanced over at my father, but tried not to let my eyes linger for fear of signaling to him that something was up. Dad didn't look like the Ricky Stevenson clone I had seen in front of me at breakfast, instead he had morphed himself back in to the ordinary presence of Jack White. Dad finished up his chicken then washed it down with a glass of skim milk. Mom had been unsuccessfully trying to get him to eat less lately because of his ever increasing spare tire. Seeing as how losing his love handles and spare tire might make him look a little too much like the world's most famous missing man I could sort of see why he had grown attached to them.

Dad cleared his throat then directed his eyes toward mine.

"Steven, I have a question for you. What happened to our large size display box on top of the hardware shelf?"

The box! In all of the excitement about finding out what was inside locker seventeen, I had completely forgotten about it. I had also forgotten to put the original key back in its hiding place. It was probably still sitting on the counter next to the key machine. Maybe Dad didn't know there was a key hidden up there; after all it looked as if it had been stuck there for years. He could have forgotten, or maybe the people who owned this place before us had put it there. I had the feeling that it was definitely not the key which had been used in the regular maintenance of the space.

"I sold it," I said "There was this guy who was clearing out space 116 and he really wanted it. I tried to get him to buy the plastic version but he was really insistent. I figured as soon as we get more in we can make a new display. I didn't want to make him unhappy, in case he needs to rent from us again."

"Oh okay I was just wondering what happened to it." Dad paused for a few seconds and his eyes seemed to brush with Mom's in an unspoken signal, before he continued.

"Do you know what happened to the key that was under the box?"

A few more seconds of silence passed and this time it was Jeanne and I who exchanged unspoken glances. My stomach was doing somersaults and the part of me that wanted to go back to my former clueless existence was growing bigger by the minute.

"I grabbed it when I was dusting up there. I thought that it would be nice to have a key so we could start renting out seventeen, but it look likes someone's already using it. In fact it's filled with some unbelievably valuable items," I told him.

"An entire life's worth," Jeanne added.

Chapter 23
It Was Bound To Come Out Sooner Or Later

Our eyes locked and my father looked somewhat like a deer trapped in headlights. He glanced toward my mother then back again at us, paused for a second then downed half the glass of milk. He then let out a sigh and said simply.

"I couldn't be him anymore."

He paused for another minute and when Jeanne started to ask something he put up his right hand in a stop gesture.

"I think we better clear up this table and head to the den where it's more comfortable because as you may have already guessed it's a long story.

We cleared the table and my father excused himself to use the bathroom. I was secretly afraid he would run like he did all those years before, but instead I looked through the doorway and saw him leaving the bathroom then heading over to the couch where he made himself comfortable.

As I helped load up the dishwasher I looked over at Mom. She didn't look surprised or shocked, but rather was her same calm regular self.

"Did you know?" I asked her.

"Of course, I have known from the beginning. I've also suspected that someday this day would come," she said as she shut the door of the dishwasher and turned it on.

Sitting down on our worn blue couch, I looked around at our den as I waited for Dad to speak. This had never been a bad little house despite the fact that the pale blue shag carpeting hadn't been in style since 1974, and the furniture was in desperate need of replacing or at least re-covering. Our bookshelves were always overflowing, there were board games in the corner, and a large brick fireplace for cold, snowy nights when we all felt like jiffy pop. It was the house of a quintessentially average American family no doubt about it. There isn't a news reporter on the face of this earth that would ever believe that this place has been the home of Ricky Stevenson himself for the past twenty-some years.

I couldn't remember the last time we were all together in the den like this. Even our dog Oreo, and cat Sanchez had curled themselves up in here. Dad reached over to Sanchez who had formed himself into a ball of tabby on top of the coffee table and scratched him behind the ears. Then he leaned back and began his story.

"Anybody who has never been famous will never understand what it's really like. It starts off great. Hundreds of girls are all focused on you, and everywhere you go people treat you like royalty. You get all the best tables at restaurants, and you've got money to burn and somebody else to take care of the bills and the responsibility. Everybody wants to be your best friend, and you get to see the world. The whole country loves you for doing just exactly what you love to do.

Then one day all of the perks suddenly seem to start wearing thin. You run out of your favorite cereal and think to yourself: why should I send the housekeeper out just to get a silly bowl of cereal? When was the last time I went inside a grocery store anyway? So you drive down to the store and the car you bought because of its speed or its style or its high pricetag is gaining you way too much attention. Every time you turn your head there is a car full of strangers pressing their heads to the glass, half of them are holding up cameras, while the others are yelling things at you. You put on your sunglasses but of course that does nothing. You remain the same famous person as before, driving the same famous car that had been featured on an album cover everyone is familiar with, only now you are wearing sunglasses." Dad paused for a second and took a sip of his water. It occurred to me that I had never even seen him wearing a pair of sunglasses.

"Once you get to the store you are not only bombarded by the people who followed you there but by the people who were at the store already," Dad continued. "Should you venture from the car and into the store everyone immediately starts chasing you while screaming Ricky, can you sign this cereal box?, Ricky can you sign this bread bag?, Ricky I loved your last album, Ricky I hated your last album, hey Ricky a bunch of us are hanging out at the Tropicadero tonight wanna come? So of course you rush out of the store promptly without getting the cereal you came in for. You want ten minutes of privacy so badly, you find yourself speeding away from the store in your way too powerful sportscar which of course promptly gets you pulled over, but hey that's okay because of course the cop recognizes you and in exchange for an autograph, he gives you a warning, not the ticket you deserve.

After getting out of the ticket you feel slightly better about your fame. This feeling lasts until the next time you dare to venture out into public be it to a restaurant, a club or whatever and the exact same pandemonium ensues. You soon find out you can only go out to the very exclusive places so that you can only be pestered by the very exclusive. Eventually you get tired of heading off to the trendiest places to pay too much for food you never liked that much in the first place. You find that you would kill for just one opportunity to go with a couple of your buddies to a Big Boy, instead of having the housekeeper bring you another lousy hamburger from yet another tony eatery off the Sunset Strip," Dad sighed, then continued.

"While you are sitting back wishing you could go get a burger with your friends, you start to realize you don't even know who the heck your friends even are anymore. Everyone you meet seems to want something from you. First they just want to hang out at your great house with your incredible pool with its waterfall. Then they want to get to know the girls you know, and before you realize it they want you to throw parties all the time. They drink all your beer, and ruin your house, which they are starting to think of as their house since they practically live there anyway. No one respects you, or anything you own anymore, because hey it's just Ricky's, he's got plenty of money.

By then you think of contacting all of your old friends who you sort of lost contact with but half of them turn into the same type of leech as your new friends while the other half have become busy with their own lives. Every time you get together you can tell that they just can't deal with all of the attention and the double takes from strangers passing by," Dad shut his eyes for a minute, maybe he was trying to picture his former life.

"So, you start taking long drives in search of that elusive town," He continued. "The one where no one has ever heard of Ricky Stevenson, but of course it doesn't exist. Even the towns too far away to get much radio reception always have a general store of some sort featuring the newest copy of some magazine with your photo on the cover. Plus you find that being in towns of less than a hundred people make you feel even more lonely and depressed than you did before, so you turn around, and head back to L.A.

Just when you think things can't ever get better they do. You meet a girl and she doesn't seem to mind your fame, or even the fact that thousands of other girls hate her for simply being with you. Suddenly being out in public isn't so bad again. You can ignore the strangers and focus on her. Everything is great or so it seems, Dad paused for a second then yelled out. "Oww, stop it." Sanchez was clawing at his arm so he shifted the cat to my sister. Jeanne was too absorbed by Dad's story to even spare a head scratch so Sanchez sulked off toward the kitchen. He was the only member of the family not riveted by the saga of Ricky Stevenson.

"You tell this girl you want this tour to be your last," Dad continued. "You want to settle down and start a family, but she says she's too young, let's give it some time. Then you hear rumors that her liking your fame was all an act. She was getting tired of the photographers, and the autograph hounds, and the screaming throngs of teenage girls and was becoming interested in another guy who wasn't loaded down by any of that baggage. You don't believe the rumors, so you head off to your tour sure that once you get back you can convince her to settle down with you and wait till eventually the mania winds down and you would become just another guy who was famous once upon a time. Then you get a phone call saying she's gone, dead in a car accident with the guy you refused to believe even existed," Dad shifted his weight on the couch and I glanced over at Mom. If she was jealous of the mysterious Elaine, she wasn't showing it.

"So once you return to California, you want to go find that guy who drove your Elaine into that tree and strangle him, but of course you can't," Dad said. "Since you are all alone still without any real friends and virtually unable to even leave your house you find other ways to escape. You find yourself going down the path that would later be followed by people like Hendrix and Belushi. You suddenly don't mind all the people at your house because you are too high or drunk to notice. Don't like hangovers? Well you don't get them if you don't stop the drinking. This pattern goes on until you wake up one day in a jail cell in Barstow, California greeted by photographers as you stumble outside into the too bright sunlight and you realize there is just no way you can continue down this road. You decide to do the only thing that will save you in the end, you decide to kill off Ricky Stevenson."

Dad cleared his throat, uncrossed his legs and announced "That kids is fame in a nutshell, now let me tell you how I ended up here."

Chapter 24
Leaving It All Behind

"After that awful night in Barstow, I started making plans." Dad continued. "I cut way back on the drinking, and tried to act as normal as possible. Not because I felt any better about the situation, but because I didn't want to tip off anyone to my real plans. I even agreed to tour that summer. Before *Drive into the Sky* came out the executives at Emcee Records had promised me they would give me a long needed break. As usual, they quickly relinquished that promise as soon as the album began to sell well. That was pretty much the final nail in the coffin. I was just so tired I honestly thought another tour would have killed me.

My original plan was only to be gone for a little while, just a couple of years or so until things blew over. I had an old friend who was a lawyer out in Chatsworth so I contacted him. It took a lot of money but he somehow managed to find a judge who would legally change my name and keep it under wraps.

I also found a small company who made motorhomes that could tow a car behind them. I had my lawyer purchase their largest model and keep it in his backyard. I also bought his old pickup truck, and whenever I had a chance I would load it up with as much stuff as possible and make a run out to Chatsworth where I deposited it inside his garage. Bit by bit my lawyer sold off the furnishings that were too large to fit inside the motorhome. My friends were evidently too drunk or stoned to notice that every time they visited something new would be missing. The only ones who would have noticed were my cook and housekeeper, but I let both of them go, using my constant tour schedule as the excuse.

Finally by June I had packed the motorhome as tightly as possible with my remaining belongings and was ready to go. I had secretly transferred most of the money to my new accounts under the name Jack White but I also had some cash stashed in the motorhome.

I had chosen the name Jack the day I stumbled away from the jail in Barstow. After the photographers dispersed, I half consciously made my way over to my car, but I realized I couldn't go anywhere without some coffee and food. Evidently the nice people involved in the greater Barstow area penal system had forgotten to order posturepedic mattresses for their beds, so I was completely exhausted. I ended up slumped in a booth across the street at a little cafe where the waitress and patrons kept bothering me for autographs.

In order to avoid making eye contact with any new customers, I found myself staring at the front cover of the cafe menu. It was a white menu with the name Jack's Cafe embossed across the front. As I looked at it, I began to wish I was just an ordinary guy named Jack. It seemed like your typical all American name. A perfect fit for an ordinary guy who did nothing but blend in.

Instead of asking "Are you Ricky Stevenson, can I have your autograph?" as loudly as possible, the waitress would simply pour my coffee and casually ask "How's your day Jack?"

I kept Richard as my middle name just in case. You never know if someone might yell it out across a crowd. If I turned around out of instinct I could just explain it away by telling people that Richard is my middle name," Dad paused for a second and drummed his fingers slightly on the armrest of the faded blue couch.

"I had thought about selling the Corvette because it was such a noticeable car, but I loved that car and I just couldn't bring myself to do it," he continued. "Instead I decided to take her with me. On the morning I left, I woke up before sunrise, gathered up the last of what I was taking, and drove over to Jamie's and Dad's where I dropped off the notes I had written. I don't remember exactly what they said, but I do remember throwing in a reference to *Another Mississippi Morning* so they would be convinced it was a suicide note. Then I headed off to Chatsworth, told my friend goodbye, put the Corvette in neutral and covered it with so many tarps and covers, it was practically mummified. I hitched her up to the motorhome, and headed off to begin my new life.

I never intended to head east, I had just put the whole bit about the Mississippi in my notes in order to throw people off. Instead I headed north up highway 99. It was a long slow journey. The motorhome was loaded down, and I didn't dare get pulled over since my driver's license still identified me as Richard Stevenson.

I spent a couple of days heading north, and stopped when I reached Chico. I only intended to spend a few weeks there but by then the story had really broken. Ricky Stevenson hadn't appeared for his first couple of tour dates and people had begun to suspect something was up. First Jamie decided to share my note with the entire world, then some sleazy photographer had managed to get pictures of my empty house. The next thing I knew every radio station I heard seemed to be having the same contest: find Ricky Stevenson and win! Remember keep your eye out for a young man in a blue and white Corvette license number CLJ 412. Emcee Records along with this station are offering a large monetary reward," Dad spoke the last few words in a cheesy radio announcer style voice, then he cleared his throat and continued telling his story in his regular speaking style.

"I ended up becoming a temporary recluse, spending the rest of the summer in a small town near Chico. I stayed in motels once I got sick of the cramped motorhome, and I let my hair and beard grow out and started packing on the pounds. My hectic schedule of constantly touring and recording had made me a pretty lean guy, but once I left that all behind, I found I gained weight pretty easily. Unfortunately, the extra pounds stuck around a bit longer than I intended," Dad chuckled.

"Once I was satisfied that I no longer looked that much like Ricky Stevenson," he continued. "I took a few small construction jobs, so I wouldn't stand out. I headed up to Oregon and rented a small apartment in Grants Pass, where I occasionally did odd jobs that were paid under the table. I stayed in Oregon a while and got myself a driver's license under my new name. I figured it was smart to have a permanent address in order to establish the history of Jack White. I was contemplating putting down even more roots there, but one day I stepped outside and saw some kids poking around the Corvette trying to get the cover off. I decided then and there it was time to go. I once again headed north. My new driver's license seemed to work just fine when it came to passing into Canada late one night.

The close call with the kids had gotten me a little bit paranoid about the car. Since my license plate number had been broadcast to almost everybody in America and possibly Canada as well, selling it no longer seemed to be an option. While driving around Vancouver one day I saw a big sign for a moving and storage company. It reminded me of the large Bekins sign I used to drive by on Ventura Boulevard at home, so when I passed it I turned around, thinking it might just fit my needs.

The moving company was run by the Daniels family. When I explained that I had inherited some items from my uncle, and I needed a place to store them, both Ted and Irene Daniels looked at me like I was crazy. They had never stored anything for an individual before, only businesses or moving companies. Since they hadn't been earning enough money and I stood before them with a wad of cash they agreed to rent me a space. On the way out I ran into their daughter Ellen."

"Your father fascinated me from the first time I met him," My mother said "He had long hair and a scraggly beard that infuriated my father. He was living in a trailer, but he only looked like a hippie on the outside. Jack seemed to have way more money than your average flower child and certainly didn't act like any of the ones I had met in Vancouver. He was polite and quiet and didn't go on and on about this issue or that one. Everything about Jack was an enigma, so of course I developed a huge crush on him."

My mother and father exchanged knowing glances then Dad returned to telling his story.

"Ellen and I became fast friends and shortly after we began dating. Since she knew I was new in town she showed me around. She was very easy to talk to. I had gotten used to girls who were only attracted to me because of my fame and money, yet here was one who, since she didn't know about either, must have been attracted to the real me.

As things grew more serious between us I thought of keeping my identity secret and asking her to marry me, but the less I told Ellen, the more guilty I felt. She had told me everything about her own life. Ellen had grown up in Indianapolis then moved up to Vancouver after high school. She missed her older brother and sister who still lived back in the States, and she had put off plans for college because the moving and storage business wasn't making a profit," Dad said. I had always wondered why my mother never went to college and now I knew.

"Finally I broke down one night and told Ellen everything," Dad continued. "I expected her to promptly break up with me and call the local radio station afterward, but instead she agreed to not only keep my secret but to marry me.

We got married later that year. Ellen's father relented after I trimmed my hair a bit, and she had convinced him that I needed to keep the beard. Shortly after the wedding your grandparents decided to sell the moving and storage company and move back to Indiana, and Ellen and I decided to come along.

We spent a few years in Indianapolis where I worked at her father's office supply store. We had never told her parents my secret figuring the less people who knew about it the better. Instead they believed I had inherited some money from my uncle who had passed away. We owned a small house just outside the city, but I was looking for a more permanent place to settle down.

I remembered Delacourte, not just because I had performed here once but because, I had a friend in high school who went to Delacourte University. I visited him here once. I remember staying in his room while he showed me around town and took me to a few parties. By then I was moderately famous, but most of the students were too busy doing their own thing to notice, and those who did were cool about it.

We played Frisbee, hung out in coffeeshops, aimlessly browsed the bookstore, and did all of the other ordinary things college students do on a daily basis. It was an experience I never had before and I relished it. That trip ended up being one of the last times I felt like a normal human being. The next time I visited Delacourte, it was for my concert so every time I left my hotel room I was greeted by the typical crush of crazed fans. I didn't get a chance to see my friend at all." This explained a lot, I thought. I had always assumed my parents' decision to move here involved a dartboard.

"Ellen was also familiar with Delacourte because her siblings had gone to school here," Dad said. "I suggested that it looked like a nice place to raise a family and she agreed. We both felt that it was time to stop working at her father's place and maybe start a business of my own. I looked into restaurants, stores, and almost any other type of business you could imagine, but none of them seemed right. Then I heard about a company who was starting a new concept, personal storage. This seemed to fit the bill nicely. Not only would Delacourte have a large base of temporary residents from which to draw, but I would have a place to keep my car and everything else that tied me to my former life. I grew quite tired of trying to explain to various house guests just why they couldn't see inside my garage.

It turned out there already was a new Stor'N'More on Highland, but the retired couple who had bought it were growing tired of the Indiana winters and agreed to sell. Ellen and I naturally did all of the moving ourselves due to the delicate nature of some of my belongings. While backing up the truck I rented, I accidentally hit seventeen causing the dent. Since seventeen was the age I had been when my first hit came out I figured it had to have been a stroke of destiny. I promptly decided to make it the place where I would store everything having to do with Ricky Stevenson."

Chapter 25
A Thousand Corvettes

After my father finished his story we sat in silence for a few minutes letting it all sink in. I had so many questions I wasn't really sure where to start. I decided to just go ahead and ask the most important one of all.

I cleared my throat and asked

"So what happens now?"

My father looked at me and answered

"Hopefully nothing."

"Nothing?" I said "You mean you want us to just keep this a secret? I mean our house is falling apart, we barely make our bills, and all the while we have stuff tucked away in one of our spaces that God himself probably doesn't the true value of."

"Actually we have never really had a problem meeting the bills," Dad said. "Your mother and I just told you kids that so you would learn the true meaning of a dollar instead of becoming spoiled brats. Though judging from the way you're acting right now, I am not sure the plan worked. Weren't you listening at all when I was talking about what it's like to be famous? Would you really like to have grown up in a house where we would be afraid to let you outside for fear of kidnappers? Where every time we go out we would be met up by a sea of paparazzi? All I ever wanted were kids who would have the opportunity to grow up free of all that, so they could figure out who they really are. So a couple of the door hinges in the place are rusty, at least now I can go down to the local hardware store and get a couple of cans of WD-40, without having to worry about being mobbed."

"This isn't going to be an easy secret to keep," I said "Aren't you worried about someone finding out?"

"Of course I am, but if anyone had the slightest clue I am sure it would have been revealed by now," he said.

"Have you ever thought that maybe it was time to tell the world the truth about who you really are. Stop living a lie. Maybe if you do it won't be so bad and after a while people will start to leave you alone," I said.

Dad was starting to get angry with me now, I could tell by the way his eyebrows began to arch, then crease up in the middle. He took a deep breath and responded.

"Jack White is not a lie; it's Ricky Stevenson who was the lie. I was never cut out to be famous, it just happened. I never asked for it. I was perfectly happy when we played to nearly empty halls and birthday parties. I was a musician because I loved singing and playing my guitar, that's all. Do you know how hard it is to give up something you love? I had no choice. I had to give up that one part of my life in order to find my true self. I was meant to be a regular guy and it's been worth it. My only regrets are that I kept anything from my prior life at all. I should have just left it all back in L.A. and gone for a truly clean slate, but no, I could never quite leave Ricky behind. I even had the gall to give my first child a shortened version of my old last name. I should have been willing to pay the price for the privilege of becoming a regular guy. I think that's worth a Corvette, hell I think it's worth a thousand Corvettes."

Dad was still glaring at me, when he finished this speech. Before I had a chance to respond my mother cut in saying

"Jack calm down, Steven is just a little overwhelmed by the whole situation."

"I am perfectly calm" he said "Anyway, since Steven is so convinced that things will be nice and calm once our friends in the tabloid world get wind of our situation. I was thinking maybe it's time for me to give them a little heads up. How's that sound, huh Steven? You still want fame and fortune don't you, well trust me kid, you soon won't."

"Jack, what on earth are you talking about?" Mom asked him.

"I will tell you later dear. Now kids if you don't mind, It's pretty late, and I think it's time for me to get to bed." Dad got up and headed upstairs, leaving Mom, Jeanne, and me with bewildered looks on our faces.

"What do we do now?" I asked Mom. "I mean it's going to be really really hard to keep this secret."

"I know kids but please do your best. When I first found out I was dying to tell people too. You just have to make an effort to push to the back of your minds. Concentrate on your own lives, pay attention to your schoolwork, get involved in more after school activities and it will become easier, trust me," she said.

"Umm I guess so, I mean I will really try," I answered.

···

I spent the next few days trying to follow my mother's advice and concentrate on anything other than Ricky Stevenson. It wasn't easy. In algebra class I sat looking down at my assignment and tried to really concentrate on the quadratic equations. Feel the equations, be the equations. What is X? I still have no clue but now I *care*. X is my friend. Oh Lord who am I fooling? I don't know what the hell X is, if I did I wouldn't be one of the only juniors stuck in a math class with mostly freshmen. Who the hell needs X when your father is a rock and roll legend?

I tried to find myself an after school activity. Sports were out since I apparently have the grace and athleticism of a drunken circus clown. Drama club might be okay except for the small fact that I was not actually enrolled in drama class. I kept thinking of Ricky Stevenson's one movie role. Ricky played Danny Beat: The main character's best friend in *Bikini Beach Barbecue*. Unlike many of the largely forgotten 60's beach genre movies, *Bikini Beach Barbecue* has become a cult phenomenon. Not for its stars, or it's plot (or lack thereof) but solely for my father's campy acting. Never before had anyone had such universally awful reviews.

I tried to absorb my teachers long winded lectures on the French and Indian War, or the life cycle of an amoeba. I took as many notes as possible, filling my pages with actual words instead of my usual doodles of guitars, Corvettes and the back of Justine Weeks's luscious head. I was now Steven White scholar at large and I was hating it.

...

This torture went on until the next Tuesday at lunch. I was sitting at our usual table trying to really pay attention to Stuart's dumb story about some prank he played on a girl during a band competition, and wondering if you could play the guitar in a high school band, when Joey walked in. He was listening to his headphones as usual, but he yanked them off and made an announcement.

"Dude. Steven you are not going to believe it. They are selling the car."

"What car?" I asked, rudely interrupting Stuart, who just kept on talking anyway.

"What car? What car do you think? Only Ricky Stevenson's Corvette. Some anonymous guy is going to sell it right here in Delacourte. They say that there is proof it's the real one. I just heard it on the radio," He responded.

"Why the hell are they selling it in Delacourte?" Dave asked

"I don't know man, but they said there is going to be some auction at the college. Until then it's going to be put on display in the university gym. We gotta go see it," Joey said.

"Oh man this totally means that Ricky Stevenson is alive. I knew it," Stuart said, finally wising up to the fact that no one cared about his band exploits.

My friends continued talking all at once and didn't seem to take notice of how uncharacteristically quiet I was being on the whole matter. I had just gone into shock. My father had decided to sell the car? Why the hell didn't he bother to tell his family about this little development? A few minutes later the bell rang and I wandered off to class slipping back into total distraction and the sheer inability to concentrate on anything. To tell the truth it felt pretty good to return to my natural state.

Chapter 26
Jack's Plan

Once I got home I wanted to confront Dad but found only Jeanne instead.

"He's off somewhere running errands I guess," she told me when I asked.

I thought of going over to seventeen to check if the car was still inside, but there were a few customers about, so I plopped down on the couch and watched one of those talk shows where everybody gets into a huge fight over who is the father of a fifteen year old's baby. Jeanne sat down on the couch beside me and asked, "Why the hell are you watching this?"

"I dunno, there's nothing else on," I responded just as a news promo came on, causing our conversation to cease.

"Tonight at five: A piece of rock and roll history is about to be auctioned off right here in Delacourte, but is it the real deal?" the newscaster said, while a stock photo of a Corvette was displayed on the screen behind her.

"Oh my God, Dad is selling the car," Jeanne said.

"Yeah my friend heard it on the radio, I am waiting for the news to get more details," I said.

We had to sit through the usual assortment of Delacourte area "news" brought to us by your friendly local news team of Cheryl Lambert and Brett Jeffers. The night's thrilling top story was about a silo fire in nearby Meridith, Indiana population: fourteen. It was followed by news of a hike in parking permit costs at the university, and the story of yet another fraternity being put on alcohol probation. By the time they got to the car auction I wondered if maybe people didn't care that much about Ricky Stevenson anymore after all.

"In other news," Cheryl said. "A California lawyer is putting a 1959 turquoise blue and white Corvette for auction claiming that it is the car owned by Ricky Stevenson, the famous musician who mysteriously vanished back in 1964. The lawyer Stan Johnson, of Los Angeles, has announced that he has proof showing the car to be genuine, and he is scheduling it to be publicly appraised by a world renowned auction house. Mr. Johnson is representing an anonymous person who has requested that the car be sold right here in Delacourte. The car itself will be up for public viewing before the sale. All profits from tickets sold for the viewing will benefit university organizations."

"Interesting story, that would be something if the car went on to be the real deal" Brett responded with an annoying chuckle before he segued into a lengthy summary on how the Delacourte University Lions were doing in lacrosse this year. I zoned off at that point, thinking Stan Johnson--where have I heard that name before?

...

Jeanne and I watched the national news but neither it or the entertainment show that followed had any stories about the upcoming car sale. At a quarter to seven Mom and Dad came home and Jeanne promptly greeted them with a cross.

"Why the heck didn't you tell us you were going to sell the car?"

Dad responded with a quick.

"Nice to see you too. It's my car to sell and I thought the profits would be handy to send you two to college, besides, it's not like we can ever drive it."

"Why do you need money to send us to college? I thought you were rich, you're Ricky Stevenson for God's sake," I said to Dad.

"Yeah, well Ricky Stevenson got married, bought himself a business, and had kids. Pretty soon all his financial security was going towards paying for Hot Wheels, E-Z Bake Ovens, eyeglass prescriptions, and orthodontic procedures. Your mother and I have some money saved, but it's not nearly as much as you might think," he responded.

"Your father's right," Mom said. "Since your father doesn't get the royalties, we don't really have that much money left from the days when he was Ricky. He and I discussed this at length the other night and we decided the Corvette isn't doing anyone any good just sitting there. It's time to let it go."

"So anyway kids, you better start bracing yourself for the media storm," Dad said.

"What media storm? It barely made the local news," I said.

"That's because the big networks haven't got wind of it just yet. Trust me it's coming," he said then looked at my outfit, which consisted of the preppiest, most generic things I own. Lately I just hadn't been into the whole Ricky vibe, for obvious reasons.

"Why the heck aren't you dressed like yourself Steven?" He asked "The last thing we want to do is call any attention to ourselves right now. You had better go back to being your normal fifties looking, Ricky Stevenson obsessed state do I make myself clear."

"I thought you hated my fifties look," I said.

"Of course I don't, you're being ridiculous. Now you better start acting very excited about the car around your friends, and whatever you do don't do anything out of the ordinary that may give our secret away. That goes for you too Jeanne," he said.

...

Despite my vocal denials, I knew the media storm was coming, and I didn't want my father's plan to blow up in his face. Well at least most of me didn't. There was a small part of me that wanted the world to know, I am not just Steven White average son of your typical family, unnoticed and seemingly headed for Dexter Community College and a life of mediocrity. No sir, I am Steven White, musical prodigy, and son of the world famous musician Richard "Ricky" Stevenson, surely destined to follow his old man into a life of stardom and worldwide appreciation.

Despite these hidden desires, I was determined that if my father's secret came out it certainly wouldn't be my fault. I was going to go back to being the same vintage clothing wearing, thrift store surfing, oldies listening Ricky Stevenson fan I had always been--even if it killed me. My father may not have been able to act but I sure could. With that oath in mind, I laid out my favorite outfit for the next day.

Chapter 27
The Frenzy Begins

By the next morning the story had pretty much broken into the national market. I had gone downstairs to grab a pop tart when I noticed my mother had left the TV on. One of the morning shows was doing a segment where weatherman Bud Louis walked around the streets of New York and asked various people about Ricky Stevenson. The first of the interviews went something like this:

Bud: "So do you consider yourself a fan of Ricky Stevenson?"

Random Guy: "yeah he's alright, I like some of his songs, but I am not one of those crazy fans who make pilgrimages to his house or anything."

Bud: "So did you hear about the plans to auction off yet another '59 Corvette that is supposed to be the one he disappeared with?"

Random Guy: "No man I didn't, seriously. I thought they did that once, but the car was some kind of a crazy fake."

Bud: "Yes that car did end up being a well done replica, but this time the seller swears he has absolute proof that this is the car which once belonged to Ricky Stevenson himself.

What I want to know this morning is what do you think: will this car be authentic?"

Random Guy: "Well yeah I think it's gotta be. I mean who would be stupid enough to try the same thing twice?"

...

I watched a couple more of these interviews until my mother came in and said "Steven get moving. You're going to be late."

"Just a second Mom, I just wanna see this one segment."

"Steven, now."

"Okay okay."

I got up and grabbed my backpack then started to head out the door, but before I officially left I remembered to ask her something.

"Is the car still here? The Corvette I mean."

"Nope, it's at the School getting prepped for the sale. From here on out if you want to see it it's going to cost you five dollars"

"Five bucks, aww come on. Anyway, how did you move it? I didn't even know it was gone."

"Let's just say it involved a large truck, your father's lawyer friend, and a lost chance for some sleep," she said stifling a yawn. "Now get going!"

"Okay okay, wait, I have a quick question."

"What is it Steven?"

"Where does Dad keep his key for seventeen? I mean the one I found was all rusted and gross. He's got to have a better one somewhere."

"Well last night when we opened up the space it was on his keychain. As far as I know that's where it's always been."

"Oh okay, I was just wondering. See you later." I responded.

My father's keychain went well beyond the car and house keys of most people. His was a tangle of keys belonging to locks which had no doubt been cut off or replaced years ago. At least that's what I had always assumed. When not in use, the keys never left Dad's pocket. In fact I suspected he put them in his pajama pockets before he went to bed, but since my parents lock their door I could never verify that theory. Whenever I needed help opening something Dad would come over and open it himself instead of just handing me the keys. I had noticed how protective of them he was, but I just figured only he knew what was what, or he didn't trust me.

I was convinced Dad thought that if I possessed his precious keys for even a second the temptation would be too much and I would take the station wagon for a joyride down Highland, blasting its AM radio all over town.

Every time I did get to borrow one of the cars I was always handed mom's set of keys. There is nothing more embarrassing than going from place to place in a huge white tank, with a keychain that features your fourth grade class picture dangling from the ignition. Oh well, I suppose it could be worse. The Stormobile could have been avocado green, or paneled with artificial wood.

...

After running back up to my room one last time to get the math book I forgot, I went outside and hopped on my bike and rode across town towards Delacourte High. While on my way I was passed by two trucks. One for *NBC News* and the other for the *Celebrities Today!* television show.

Heading north from the Stor'N'More, you get to the High School before you come to the University so I couldn't see if things had yet evolved into a full blown media frenzy. I didn't want to go to school at all. I considered cutting, but I remembered that Dave said that there might be a pop quiz in history and I couldn't afford to miss another one.

As I walked into first period English class I felt all eyes on me. Maybe it was just because I was ten minutes late, but

I had a definite feeling it was because of my Ricky Stevenson similarity. I turned toward Justine's side of the room and gave them my best impersonation of a rock star smile before taking my seat.

"Psst, Steven," Joey said after poking me squarely in the back.

"What?"

"Are you going tonight?"

"What's tonight?"

"They are showing off the car starting tonight at five, in the university gym. It's only five bucks a pop."

"Oh yeah, sure. I didn't know they were showing it tonight."

"Yeah I heard this morning on my radio. You want to meet up and go together?"

"Umm whatever you guys were gonna do is fine with me."

Mr. Sloan cleared his throat and since we knew he would give us detention if we let out another peep, so we nodded to each other as a silent signal to finish our conversation after class.

While walking throughout the hallowed halls of Delacourte High School I definitely felt more eyes than usual on me. Was this what my father was talking about when he talked about fame? If it was the man was completely off his rocker. This was great, more than great. Did Dan Parker just wave to me? Nah I must be hallucinating.

I headed toward my locker when I was stopped by Dave who said: "Everybody's going over to my house after school because I live pretty near the university gym. Then we are going to get in line to see the car. You in?"

"Of course," I told him

"Okay, good deal. See you then."

"Dave, wait."

"What?"

"Did you cut through the university on your way to school? Was it busy at all? I saw a news van on my way here."

"Oh yeah I saw a couple of reporters around and I wanted to stop and do an interview, but I had to get to school because I have History first period and I didn't want to miss the pop quiz."

"So there is a pop quiz."

"Yeah, but it wasn't that hard, thank God."

...

After school we only stopped briefly at Dave's house before heading to the gym where a very long line was starting to form. Several refreshment tables had been set up alongside our path, and the Alpha Beta Upsilon fraternity had somehow managed to have the honor of being the first to create a T-shirt for the occasion. The shirts had a cartoon on them featuring a caricature of Ricky sitting on the hood of the Corvette in between two bikini clad buxom blondes. The lettering underneath read *I saw Rick's Rockin 'Vette in Delacourte Indiana*. My father would be so proud.

My favorite radio station *Rockin Oldies 101* was there belting out Ricky Stevenson songs while DJ "Whatcha Gonna Do Stu?" Clark was giving out T-shirts and gift certificates to those who knew the answers to Ricky Trivia. I knew most of the answers but good ole Stu didn't seem to hear my responses. Finally Joey started belting out whatever I said at the top of his lungs. His copied response to what was the name of Ricky's beloved guitar finally got Stu's attention and he came this way.

"Alright we have a winner of a free small yogurt at the Yogurt Palace who just gave the correct answer of Lu Lu Mae?"

My friends all pointed towards me, and DJ Stu gave out a big grin.

"Hey I remember you. It's Steven White, right?"

"Uhh yeah that's me."

"Stand up Steven. Ladies and gentlemen, I would like to introduce last summer's winner of the Ricky Stevenson look-alike contest, held last summer in honor of the 30th anniversary of his disappearance. I was wondering when you were going to show up. You wouldn't miss this for the world would you Steve?"

"Nope I guess I wouldn't," I told Stu.

I let out a small grin, this was starting to get embarrassing. Not only were everybody's eyes were on me but one of the local TV stations seemed to be filming the whole thing. Then Dan Parker or someone from that whole popular clique belted out "Way to go Steve!" and I felt better.

"Well it's good to have you here, though I do admit it's a bit disappointing that you didn't wear your grand prize *Rockin Oldies 101* jacket for this occasion," Stu said.

"Umm, well I was worried it might rain. I don't want to ruin it," I responded.

The jacket in question had to be the ugliest item of clothing ever made. It was a grotesque leather number, with garish cloth sleeves. Each of the sleeves was a different color one bright red, the other bright blue, and the back of the jacket was completely covered in the *Rockin Oldies 101* logo done up in hot pink and neon green. I couldn't help but wonder what I might have won had I lived in a somewhat larger radio market.

Just then Joey cleared his throat and said "Seeing as how Steve is Delacourte's official Ricky Stevenson look-alike do you think he could have the privilege of having his picture taken with his friends inside the car?"

"Yeah how about it?" my other friends promptly chimed in.

"Sorry I'm afraid not. If I did Ricky Stevenson just might come out of hiding and pummel me personally," Stu chuckled as he handed me a coupon. "Enjoy your free yogurt, courtesy of our friends from the Yogurt Palace with their two convenient locations right here in Delacourte. Now who can tell me the name of the city where Ricky went to High School?"

At five o'clock sharp the doors to the gym opened and the first group of people was admitted. Our group went inside fifteen minutes later. The Corvette looked incredible, not that it looked so bad in seventeen, just a little dusty. Now it looked as if fourteen coats of waxes and lacquers had been applied. It was lit up on all sides and underneath by alternating white and purple lights and we were separated from it only by a velvet rope.

"Wow it's beautiful, I would definitely drive it." Stuart said as he took several pictures ignoring the *no flash photography* signs posted everywhere.

"Mmmm smooth," Joey said petting the exterior.

"Hey don't touch it--do you want that guard over there to kick us out?" Dave whispered to him.

Joey ignored Dave and turned to me saying, "I dare you to sit in it. I'll give you twenty bucks."

"I'm not going to sit in it, there is a guard right there," I whispered back.

"What about for fifty bucks."

"NO!"

"I'll sit in it for fifty bucks."

"Joey."

"What?"

"Shut up! No one is sitting in the car."

The guard cleared his throat "All right kids, times up. We have a lot more people waiting to get in. Also I heard what you were saying about sitting in the car. Don't even think about it. And you NO FLASH PHOTOGRAPHY! Got that?"

"I'm sorry, my flash is automatic and anyway it's for my school paper," Stuart responded.

Joey met the guards gaze and asked, "for fifty bucks will you let my friend sit in the car while we take a photo? He's

Ricky's biggest fan and I think he's dying. No one will know, come on."

"Absolutely not, now leave before I lift each of you up and throw you out." was the guard's response.

As we left I wished I could have told my friends that not only had I had sat in the Corvette's driver seat, but the passenger seat as well. I wanted to brag about how I had rifled through the glove compartment, found the keys and opened up and investigated the trunk. But of course I couldn't tell them any of it. Life is so unfair.

Chapter 28
Ricky Mania

It was lucky we went to see the car when we did because now the line is stretching through the entire city of Delacourte. At least that's the case if you believe *Celebrities Today! Entertainment Connection, Hollywood Weekly*, or any of the other tabloid television shows that have now camped themselves here.

Ever since that one fateful day in eighth grade, I spent my entire life feeling isolated in my love for all things Ricky Stevenson. Sure from time to time, I would play my Ricky and the Sleepers' albums for various friends and they would claim to like them, but to my knowledge they never went home and bought themselves a copy of the greatest hits collection. Instead my friends went back to listening to whatever musical style was the flavor of that month. I was simply never able to convert anyone into become a Ricky disciple like myself. Even Greg Lewis with his innate sense of whatever retro fad was coming back into style, didn't seem to care one way or another about Ricky Stevenson.

None of this actually mattered to me however. Let my friends go and pay 14 bucks a CD for whatever flannel grunge, teen pop, or heavy metal rap act was big that week. In my mind Ricky Stevenson was a classic, whether or not anyone else saw it that way. So what if I had different taste in music and clothes than most of the annoying preppy kids who go to my school. I was different and I was proud of it.

At least I was different until a couple of days ago. From the looks of it every single student at Delacourte High had suddenly become a huge Ricky Stevenson fan. All of a sudden the popular kids were coming to me for advice. A constant stream of questions seemed to bounce towards me as I would walk down the halls. It seemed like I couldn't go a day without hearing.

"Hey Steve, where's a good place to get that vintage look?" or

"Hey Steven by any chance do you know what that stuff Ricky used in his hair was?"

My responses were usually short as I recalled them pretty much verbatim from the various magazine articles, television shows, and Ricky books I had read over the years. I was getting rather tired of saying "I read somewhere that Ricky's guitar was a Les Paul," when what I wanted to tell my more popular classmates went something like this.

"You know I have actually strummed the 1958 custom Les Paul with a sunburst finish that belongs to Ricky Stevenson himself. Swear to God. I would have plugged it into the amp, but it's in a storage space and I didn't know if the plugs were working and I didn't want to risk it with a guitar and amplifier that are over thirty years and potentially worth millions. Oh and umm if Ricky himself ever found out, I think he would ground me."

Or

"Last night Ricky Stevenson, who has been my idol for practically my entire life came up to my room, sat down on my bed and taught me some of his tips and tricks for playing the guitar. I never quite got the chords right on *Lanie Lanie* 'till he showed me. Then he informed me that I inherited my mother's hands."

Of course the popular kids didn't need to know that I have unearthed Ricky Stevenson's secret identity. Just looking like him was currently enough to attain instant popularity. Out of the blue I was invited to not one but three popular kid's parties and Mike Collins told me that Jenny Campbell's brother wanted me to play Ricky Stevenson in a skit for his college fraternity.

Outside of school I blended in with what seemed like thousands of Ricky Stevenson tribute artists who had flooded our city. Old, young, white, black, male, female, my father seemed to have almost as large a following as Elvis himself.

I had already sensed this onslaught was coming of course. Ricky Stevenson could not have had two movies about his life, three tribute albums, thousands of collectibles, hundreds of fan clubs, and countless stories on television shows if people didn't still care about him 30 years later. This said, it was a whole different experience seeing the phenomenon up close, than sitting alone watching yet another episode of *Famous Mysteries* on the *Celeb! Network*.

It was weird being surrounded by all things Ricky. Not only was he on the lips of everyone in town, but almost every downtown business had followed in the footsteps of the Alpha Betas and produced a Ricky Stevenson T-shirt of some kind. Huge posters of the 1962 era Ricky now graced the University Gym as well as a great many other buildings around town. There were stories in all of the local papers about all the revenue the Ricky Stevenson mania was bringing into Delacourte's chronically troubled downtown. The university paper the *Delacourter* even had the headline: *Thank You Ricky Wherever You Are*.

With all the chaos around town most of us locals were ignored, even me. Despite my retro wardrobe, inherited Ricky-ness, and valiant efforts by my friends and other members of Delacourte High's newly formed Ricky Stevenson Fan Club I was unable to get noticed by any of the television shows or news reporters who had come here. A local kid with a resemblance to Ricky evidently was just not nearly as interesting as most of the visitors who had converged on Delacourte. They were just too busy doing fluff pieces on a motorcycle gang of oldies music aficionados who had biked here from L.A., a Philadelphia mother who claimed that the music of Ricky Stevenson had made a significant breakthrough in her autistic son, and a psychic who now claimed that Ricky was alive and well and living alone in a large mansion just outside of New Haven, Connecticut.

Chapter 29
A Lot of Fried Chicken and a Little Eavesdropping

Thursday night my father took us all to dinner. Seeing as how pundits were predicting the Corvette would reach record prices you would think he would take out his family to the nicest place in town, but no, as usual we ended up at Jay's Family Style buffet.

Never in the history of our city had Jay's been so full. I can't even ever remember seeing a line that lasted more than five minutes, before you were allowed to go in and gorge yourself. Now that the world's eye had fallen upon our humble little 'burg, there was a major wait. We got in line and found ourselves standing behind a group of Ricky impersonators (along with one lone Elvis, hey every group needs a rebel), some sort of a church group wearing matching poorly silk-screened *God loves Ricky* t-shirts, and various people affiliated with the numerous TV enterprises that had descended upon Delacourte. The TV reporters and such were the most vocal about their displeasure at having to eat at a buffet. As we were waiting for a table, I strained to overhear the various snippets of conversation that floated around me.

"Why the hell does this person want to sell the car in the Midwest, for God's sake Marty. I mean it would have such a better reception if the auction took place in New York. I heard that Maggie herself is just having an absolute fit over the whole thing, and who can blame her." one of them was saying.

Another was having an animated conversation with her cellphone.

"Lord, I have had more beef in the past week than I have had in the last year, Every decent restaurant in this town is just mobbed I am at a buffet for heaven's sake, plus there is not one single place to get a decent latte. If Ricky himself was really alive, I know they would hold the auction back in a normal place like Beverly Hills."

This woman must have completely missed downtown Delacourte and its adjacent university during her jaunts through our little city. How else could she have possibly missed the fact that there were three coffeehouses within a radius of two blocks. Average Joe's, Mocha's on Main, and Summa Cum Latte. Not to mention the Delacourte Lions athletic boosters coffee cart set up on campus.

When we were finally seated, I made my way towards the fried chicken and had to squeeze between two heavyset men in tacky shirts who were involved in a conversation. Both men were oblivious to the fact that, yes, there were actually hungry people in this restaurant who may just like to partake of said chicken.

"This is a good lead I just know it," one of them said. "I mean the guy's a loner and a millionaire and he lives out in the middle of frikin Nowheres-ville, what did you say the name of that town was again Lee?"

"Uhhh Monroeville or Monroeburg something like that," Lee responded.

"Yeah anyway I think this guy has got to be Ricky. Call it a hunch but I've been right before haven't I? We gotta bring along Marco for pictures, maybe we can get the inside of the garage, you know where the car used to be," The other one said.

"No, No way, man. I am not doing any breaking and entering just for a story. Look what happened to Roy."

"Come on, Roy got off with a misdemeanor and we broke that Ellie Carpenter story before anybody. Do you really want the damn *World Wide News* to get this one before us?"

Lee looked from side to side then said, "maybe we should go sit down and shut up now. I just know those *World Wide* spy bastards are everywhere."

"Yeah maybe you're right, let's go," his partner responded and they walked off.

...

"You sure took long enough to just get some fried chicken," Jeanne said as I sat down.

"Yeah well in case you haven't noticed this restaurant is just little bit busy" I responded then dove in to the chicken.

As I sipped my soda, I looked around. No one in the restaurant was taking any notice of us whatsoever. We were just another average local family. The father a bit overweight from eating at places like this, the mother pretty, but perpetually tired looking, and the kids acting immature and arguing over chicken despite the fact that they were both teenagers.

These people were way too busy, and self-involved to notice us. They chatted on their phones or impatiently tapped their feet as a reminder that they had more important things on their minds. Their anxious moods probably stemmed from the fact that the Corvette was scheduled to be appraised at 11:30 the next day. By the next afternoon they would know if this was another huge hoax or if Stan Johnson's proof would be enough. Stan himself was also making news because he had not been seen much since the car was put on display. No doubt, these reporters were drooling over the prospect of getting him alone for a televised interview.

...

After we all piled into the car my father let out a sigh then grinned.

"Can you believe it? No one noticed. Everybody in this town is talking about Ricky Stevenson but they have no clue, absolutely no idea that he's right here in front of them. Heck I even overheard a conversation about some poor rich hermit in Monroeville that they think is me. I sorta feel sorry about the poor S.O.B., tomorrow he's in for quite a surprise." Dad paused as a different group of Ricky wannabes crossed in front of our station wagon, then continued.

"Hey look at that one--not bad, not bad at all. He looks a lot more like Ricky than I do. Hey buddy, you want the fame? Well you can have it. Look there are some more clueless reporters. Hey, you schmuks, you have no idea it's me do you? Well good, go invade someone else's privacy."

"I think they don't realize you're Ricky 'cause you forgot to get valet parking for the station wagon," I told him.

"Ha ha, good one Steven, come on let's go home," he responded.

Chapter 30
The Appraisal

"No. You cannot stay home from school today," Mom told me the next morning. "You know the car is real, so why do you need to see it get appraised anyway? You don't see me just taking a day off from work do you? I haven't been able to find a decent parking spot since this whole mess started. I might as well just walk to work from here."

I had wanted to take a "mental health day" in order to see the reactions of everybody when the VIN Number ended up matching the one supplied by the dealership who sold Ricky his car. I was also curious about Stan Johnson, the lawyer who had known Dad's secret all along. I could just go ahead and cut but I had the feeling that my father might decide to risk seeing the appraisal for himself and he would kill me if he saw me there, so I had no choice but to trudge off to school, while my VCR was set to record all the action.

My poor VCR had been going through hell as I tried to record as much information about the impending car sale as I could. It started making a scary creaky noise when it rewinds and I was afraid it would start eating the tapes altogether. After school I decided to go check Highland thrift and see if they have a cheap rewinder or maybe another VCR. It had been awhile since I shopped there. The saleslady who always squints and scowls at me probably thinks I died.

···

After school I decided the thrift store could wait and instead I went directly home to watch my tape. All day at school I kept thinking: what if the numbers somehow don't match? What if the dealership supplied the wrong VIN by mistake? What if my father wasn't really Ricky Stevenson but yet another con artist who had managed to cruelly scam his own young son? Once I got home and played the tape my fears dissolved as I saw that the car was deemed authentic by Margaret Winters, an employee of the auction house. The matching VIN numbers were further substantiated by an old registration slip and a California driver's license for a Richard M. Stevenson found in the glove compartment.

I got my first look at Stan Johnson, who was standing next to the car the whole time. He was nodding a lot but not saying much of anything. Stan looked to be a little older than Dad. He had thick blonde hair, and was wearing a three piece suit and holding a briefcase. He didn't crack a smile the whole time.

Once the appraisal was over, mobs of reporters started asking him about who the current owner was, and whether or not he knew if Ricky was still alive. Stan answered "no comment" to every single question thrown his way before he got into the back seat of a Lincoln with tinted windows. The car quickly weaved its way around the throngs of unsatisfied journalists, and then drove off down Second Street.

By the time seven o'clock rolled around I planned on flipping between the various entertainment shows that come on, but my father yelled at me to shut off the TV and do my homework or else. Once again I had to give my VCR yet another strenuous workout. I swear I spent all my money lately on blank tapes.

The bulk of my homework was made up of algebra so of course it took me all night to complete. Once I was finally done I turned on the TV but my father heard it, popped his head in the door and told me to go to bed.

The next morning I was running late to school as usual, but that didn't stop me from checking out all the headlines in the newspaper bins in front of The Waffle Nook downtown. The four I saw read: *REAL DEAL, Rock and Roll History is Made, Stevenson Car Authentic,* and *The Genuine Article.*

Chapter 31
Jamie Underwood Comes To Town

I used to be able to videotape almost every show about Ricky Stevenson, slap a label on the tape and place it in my footlocker for future viewings, but that was before the Delacourte area cable system became all Ricky all the time. Nothing used to cure the blues better for me than my own private viewing of *Ricky Exposed!* or *Rock and Roll Runaway: The Ricky Stevenson Story.*

After the auction announcement, everything was different yet I still felt compelled to record as much as I possibly could. No matter how much I would tape, it barely scratched the surface. This was especially inconvenient since I have no idea how to record one show and watch another at the same time. (Thrift store VCRs do not come with manuals, you know.) With my TV always busy recording, I found myself having to watch the downstairs one alongside my family.

This hasn't actually been enjoyable since I was about ten. How could I enjoy the guilty pleasures of something like a *Dukes of Hazzard* tribute show with my mother constantly making comments about the acting skills of each Duke and the lack of a story that makes any sense whatsoever? As if that's not bad enough, on the other end of the couch, sits the even bigger distraction known as my father. How can I possibly concentrate on this riveting program when Dad keeps watching my reactions to Daisy from the corner of his eye. I mean come on its *Daisy*, short short wearing, Jeep maneuvering goddess of the early eighties. How does he think I will respond?

My mother had apparently overdosed on Ricky Stevenson mania so whenever Dad was downstairs she was usually up in the master bedroom watching an old *Murder She Wrote* or some corny movie from 1955. Jeanne and I are fans of neither so this meant if we wanted to watch some TV we were stuck downstairs with Dad.

With all the Ricky Stevenson hoopla I would have thought my father would want to avoid the television altogether, or only watch PBS shows on Egyptian hieroglyphics, or perhaps that local channel that plays community events and school lunch menus. Nope, I thought wrong. Dad had taken up watching every single Ricky Stevenson news segment, TV movie, and biography special he possibly could. He was addicted to those top ten Ricky Stevenson inspired song lists the music channels kept playing. Dad now relished the television as if it was one big inside joke, and he was the only one who got it. I would often come downstairs only to find him in front of the TV chuckling to himself and muttering phrases at it like; "yeah not quite" or "if you only knew."

One day he saw me watching a replay of *Rock and Roll Runaway*, I expected him to ask me to shut it off and do my homework like he used to, but instead he plopped down next to me.

"God I haven't seen this in ages. It's terrible. I can't believe that guy got nominated for an Oscar, he's not the least bit believable as me. He's way too blond. I never cut it as a blond." Dad said.

"You were a blond?" I asked him.

"For a few weeks when I was in Oregon, I was so desperate to not look like Ricky Stevenson I went and bought myself a bottle of dye. The stuff fried my hair and the color was awful. It certainly didn't turn my hair the shade on the box, instead it was more orange than blond. I finally figured it made me stand out even more and re-dyed my hair brown, damaging it further. I wore an awful lot of caps that year. Who knows, maybe it wasn't even the dye's fault. Stevenson's have never had the complexions for blond hair. Why do you think I didn't want Jeanne to lighten hers?" he said.

"You know I heard somewhere that Elvis was really a blond," I told him.

"I've heard that too. Can't picture it," Dad said.

I turned my attention back to the movie until the next commercial break came on.

"Is this movie realistic?" I asked. "I mean did you really get mad at your dad and play guitar on a roof all night."

"That part's not. If I pulled at stunt like that my father would have probably killed me on the spot. I did play sometimes to just to tee him off, but never to the extreme this movie claims," he said.

"What about the rest of the movie? Is any of it realistic?" I asked.

"Some parts are pretty true, others are exaggerations, and some of it they just made up. To tell you the truth Steven, some of the things may really have happened, and I don't even remember. I did some pretty stupid things back then. I tried some drugs, but I never did as many as you might think, that trend came after I disappeared. What I did do was drink way too much. There are a lot of nights I don't remember and never will. I should have given it up completely. I did for a while, but being the only non-drinker in the room makes you stand out, and my goal in life is to become totally unnoticed, so I learned to nurse my beers. I haven't had more than two drinks in one night in over 25 years," he said.

"Really?"

"Have you ever seen me drink more than two beers in a sitting?"

"I never really noticed."

"Exactly," he said.

"Oh and by the way, Steven."

"What?"

"If you ever try any of the stupid things I did back then, I will hurt you. You do know this right?"

"Yes I know."

"Okay good, now watch the movie. This part's hilarious."

...

A couple of nights after the Corvette was deemed authentic, the news was replaying the arrival of Jamie Underwood at the airport in Indianapolis. Jamie had been the drummer of Ricky and the Sleepers during their heyday. Shortly after Ricky's disappearance he had switched from drummer to lead singer while his brother, Mark had taken over as drummer. Together Jamie, Mark and the rest of the band members renamed themselves The Deep Sleepers. The band's fans were in an uproar that Jamie had taken over the reins so quickly, while the critics lambasted his singing and claimed that the band had lost its soul without Ricky. The Deep Sleepers album was a major disappointment and they were unceremoniously dropped by the Emcee label shortly after it was released.

Despite this setback, the band continued to go on various tours around the country. The considerable profit from royalties on the old Ricky and the Sleepers albums and the slew of album re-releases, books, movies, and other Sleepers memorabilia products, made Bobby Jenkins, Carl Hansen, and Jamie Underwood each a millionaire several times over.

Shortly after Ricky Stevenson bought his Corvette, Jamie bought himself the identical model only in red and white. Clearly one Corvette wasn't enough for Jamie however, because he had landed in Indianapolis in order to make a bid on Ricky's.

Jamie Underwood had a phony tan and an even more phony smile. He looked like he was trying to emulate old black and white footage of the rich and famous when they would walk down the stairs at an airport to greet their fans. Too bad the airport didn't have stairs leading from the plane, only one of those tunnels leading into the terminal. When Jamie stepped out the fluorescent lighting made his tan look orange and showed off the gray roots of his dyed blond hair.

"I have come personally to bid on the car," he told the waiting crowd, "because I really believe my old friend, Ricky, would have wanted it to stay in the Sleepers' family."

"Actually Jamie I couldn't care less," my father said to the TV, "but if you want to bid on it, hey be my guest." Then he muttered, "it's good to see you haven't changed a bit."

"You don't like him do you?" I asked.

"I didn't say that, I was actually pretty good friends with him, but nobody likes Jamie more than Jamie. He always loved attention and hated the fact that the bulk of it went to me. Jamie always had to be the star, and if it were up to me he would have been, but things didn't work out that way. That was mostly due to the fact that he never could sing worth a damn, and he never learned the guitar," Dad said.

...

Once Jamie arrived in Delacourte he was all over the TV, soaking in all the attention like a giant sponge. He posed by the car, and was seen at various spots around town often followed by an entourage, a throng of screaming college girls, or the usual assortment of Ricky fanatics begging for autographs.

I was downtown heading to Academy Thrift when I first saw him in person. Despite the fact that he was surrounded by a large group of autograph hounds, Jamie himself was easy to spot because he was the only person silly enough to have a fake tan in November in Indiana. I thought of trying to get an autograph myself, but the crowds were stifling so I headed off to the store instead.

I was flipping through the shirts when I heard the back door open. I instinctively looked up because no one ever uses the back door at Academy. I was expecting a cacophony of alarm bells to go off. Instead I saw a disheveled looking Jamie Underwood step inside and glance backwards to make sure he wasn't being followed. Jamie Underwood trying to get away from his public? Would wonders never cease? Jamie then proceeded towards the tallest nearby rack which happened to be men's' shirts, where I was standing.

"You look so much like a young Ricky Stevenson-it's spooky. It's like I have stepped back in time," he said upon seeing me.

"You've probably heard that your whole life, haven't you? That's why you are here, but you're not like most of those jokers out there trying to be impersonators, no matter what you do, you would still look like Ricky."

"Um yeah, I guess so," I said.

"Are you a tribute artist?" he asked.

"No not really, I mean I'm still in high school."

"Maybe that's why you look so much like him. People forget he was only seventeen when we had our first hit. If you wanted to be, you would make a really good Ricky tribute artist. You might even make some money from it, but if you want my advice--don't."

"Don't what?"

"Don't capitalize on it, don't try to be famous, especially not famous from being associated with someone else. Take me for example; I am only famous because I was in a band with Ricky. Don't get me wrong I love the attention, but I have always wondered why people can't like me for being Jamie, not the guy who once played with Ricky Stevenson. The truth is I am so used to being the drummer from Ricky and the Sleepers I don't really know who the real Jamie is anymore. Not that it matters. No one ever gave a damn about the real Jamie. That's what would happen to you, you would be only known as the kid who looks like Ricky Stevenson. You're not Ricky Stevenson, always remember that. Never let go of who you are. What's your name?"

"Steve."

"You should always be Steve, okay?"

"Okay."

"Sometimes I think Ricky had the right idea driving into that river." Jamie's voice began to grow distant, but I brought him back to reality by saying.

"Umm, I don't think he actually drove into the river since the car's being auctioned off. I mean that Corvette doesn't look like it's been underwater to me."

"Yes, good point. For a second there I forgot why I was here in the first place. Hell, he may even be alive. For the past thirty years I have been totally convinced Ricky Stevenson was dead, and now he could actually be alive. I simply can't fathom it. I wonder if I saw Ricky today, would I recognize him? What would I say? Would I forgive him or would I punch his lights out? I don't know," Jamie looked me over again and said

"What about you? Do you think Ricky is alive?"

Yes in fact I think he is my living room watching a game show at this very moment, asking Mom when dinner will be ready.

"I guess he could be, I'm not really sure," I said then started to ask him a question. "Umm, Mr. Underwood?"

"Jamie, nobody calls me Mr. Underwood."

"Jamie, could I have an autograph?"

"Oh, of course."

Once our bizarre conversation was complete, I hopped on my bike and headed home with my new purchase, a pale green button down shirt complete with the autographed inscription that read: *Steve, You look an awful lot like my friend*

Ricky but never forget to be yourself--Jamie Underwood. Jamie had scrawled it with a permanent marker loaned to us by the college student who managed Academy Thrift. When I left Jamie had been busy signing a different shirt for him.

Chapter 32
The Corvette and The Mystery Woman

On Wednesday before the car was due to be auctioned, the sale hit a major roadblock, when a lawyer announced that he was filing an injunction to stop the auction. The lawyer, Peter Goldbaum, was one of the most prominent attorneys in Los Angeles, and had represented Emcee records in the 1960's. Now he worked for Robert Stevenson, father of Ricky, and president of Ricky Stevenson Enterprises.

I heard about this development while flipping channels. When it comes to Ricky Stevenson, there must be an unspoken rule: every time anything is announced about him it must be done in front of as large of an audience as possible. Goldbaum held his press conference shortly after landing his private jet at Delacourte's small airport. He announced that he was filing the injunction to stop the auction because the matter of who the car belonged had not been resolved. According to Mr. Goldbaum, if the car was in Ricky's name, it belonged to Ricky's only heir, his father Robert. Unless of course, Ricky himself decided to come forward.

Upon hearing this news I switched off the TV and went into the office where I found my father going through some files and started to tell him what I had just seen.

"I know, I just heard the press conference on the radio," he interrupted me, "but don't worry, I've got it covered just wait till Stan holds his press conference at 5:30."

"But what if the judge rules that they get the profits from the sale?" I asked. "Are you going to reveal your identity?"

"I won't need to do that Steve, Don't worry, just watch."

...

At 5:30 we were all in the den, even Mom had taken a break from watching endless repeats of *The Golden Girls* and making her oven baked pork chops in order to watch the press conference.

Stan Johnson was holding his conference in front of Delacourte University's law school building. From the looks of it he had flown in the rest of his legal team or maybe he had just gathered up some well-dressed law students to give himself that aura of importance. Either way he didn't look the least bit ruffled by the earlier announcement. Unlike during the Corvette's appraisal Stan was smiling, revealing to the world a set of disturbingly perfect teeth.

I couldn't help but compare Stan Johnson to Jamie Underwood. Stan was also blonde and tan, but his tan looked as if had come from endless rounds of golf and his hair looked like it was his natural color. Maybe he touched it up from time to time but at least it blended well with his coloring. Stan had the aura of the big man on campus all grown up. He must have been a former college football player or tennis champ. Either way the man radiated success.

Stan Johnson looked like the type who should be the avid collector of classic automobiles. This made it somewhat ironic that the car in question was owned by a man who exemplified average-ness and was coveted by a has-been who was unsuccessfully attempting to cling to his youth. Jamie was so afraid to surrender to middle age that he would risk looking like a buffoon if it meant that people knew that he had once been famous.

Jamie Underwood might have been a multi-millionaire who could afford to collect sportscars, but I couldn't help but feel a little sorry for him. It can't be fun thinking of yourself as a star but always being relegated to second banana. Despite the numerous girlfriends, and screaming fans, Jamie also must have needed someone to actually talk to. After all, he had divulged a little too much of his inner self to me, a kid he just met. I think I reminded Jamie, that despite their differences, Ricky and he used to be friends. Maybe I should introduce him to Mr. Carmichael, guidance counselor extraordinaire. I could picture the two of them at a new age conference for men, baring their souls and searching for the inner meaning in Jamie's constant quest for the ultimate Corvette.

...

After a series of commercials reminded me that the possible revelation of my father's secret and impending dissolution of the White family was brought to me by Nelson Oldsmobile, and The Yogurt Palace respectively, the press conference was finally ready to begin. Stan stood in front of the bank of microphones and cleared his throat, then he calmly gazed over the crowd of reporters and announced:

"As you know this afternoon the question of ownership of the car once belonging to Richard M. Stevenson, better known as Ricky, was brought up by an attorney for the firm Goldbaum, Straub, and Long. Since that announcement was made I have been in contact with Mr. Goldbaum and have told him what I am about to tell you. The car is no longer a possession of Ricky Stevenson, but was legally transferred many years ago by Mr. Stevenson to my client who has asked to remain anonymous."

Upon hearing this news, numerous thoughts began to fill my brain.

Was this anonymous client Jack White? Had my father transferred the deed over to himself? Was that even legal? Or did he trust his lawyer that much? Was Stan Johnson the name on the pink slip, and what if he decided he wanted the money for himself? This train of thought was shortly interrupted by a reporter who asked one of the same questions currently rolling around in my head.

"Mr. Johnson could this mystery person be Ricky Stevenson using another name?" She asked.

Johnson smiled and responded.

"I have met with my client several times and I can assure you that is definitely not a possibility. Not only does my client bear no resemblance to Ricky Stevenson, there is also the small fact that she is a woman." The crowd chuckled at the statement before more of their questions began to fly.

"Mr. Johnson how does this woman still know Ricky? Was she his lover?" one of the reporters asked.

"I am not sure," he said.

"Is this woman a local of the Delacourte area?" asked another.

"I can't comment on that."

"How old is she?"

"I can't comment on that either."

"Does she know if Ricky is still alive?"

"Is she Ricky's wife or a relative?"

"Why is she selling the car?"

"I am afraid my client has requested total anonymity, which I have to respect. Perhaps after the auction, she will come forward and tell her story whatever that may be, but as for now I am afraid I cannot comment on any of these questions," Stan responded. He concluded the press conference by telling everyone the auction would go ahead as planned.

Now it was my mother's turn to chuckle at the television. She turned to Jeanne and me and winked, "bet you kids didn't know I was an avid collector of classic cars--you guys probably thought I only liked station wagons and Buicks."

...

"So why did you give the Corvette to Mom?" I asked Dad at dinner.

"With all of the hoopla around my disappearance I soon figured it was worth more than your ordinary car. I transferred the deed over to Ellen shortly before we got married. At the time I hadn't been gone that long so Ricky was still officially alive, and everything was legal. Anyway in case the marriage didn't work out, I figured I had better find a way to prevent Ellen from selling the story to the tabloids or writing a book, so I gave her the car in return for an oath that she would do neither." he said.

"I was a little miffed that Jack didn't trust me that much, but on the other hand it is a really nice classic Corvette," Mom said giving us her nauseating--I am so in love with your big lug of a father--look. She must be in order to put up with living at a storage locker emporium, while knowing full well we could have had a mansion in Beverly Hills.

Chapter 33
Who is Ricky Stevenson?

It didn't take much time for the Corvette ownership news to hit the tabloids and when it did I spent the morning in Wahl's drug glancing at them all. Every sleazy magazine had managed to somehow rush out a story on Ricky Stevenson's "mystery woman" *Take My Car--Dying Ricky's Last Wish!* read one. *Mafia Princess kills Ricky Stevenson and takes his car!* and *Ricky's Secret Lover Sells Car to Pay Medical Bills--rare cancer forcing me to sell my prized possession--Midwest housewife reveals*, were the headlines of two others. (I personally think Dad should frame the one that reads *Ricky had a Sex Change: Mexican Surgeon Reveals All!*) Our own local paper the *Delacourte Press* had the headline: *Mystery Woman Owns Ricky's Car: several television programs offering top dollar for her story*-see page one of entertainment section.

As if the mystery woman story wasn't enough, an intrepid reporter from everybody's favorite tabloid television show: *Secrets Today*, had done a profile on Stan Johnson. Stan turned out to be the older brother of Ben Johnson, a high school friend of Ricky Stevenson. Ben must have been a pretty good friend because he brushed off the onslaught of tabloid reporters that had temporarily set up camp outside of his San Diego house.

This news seemed to convince every man, woman, and child within the city limits of Delacourte that Ricky himself was somewhere among us. Suddenly every male teacher was being scrutinized by the Delacourte High student body.

"I swear Mr. Cummings has the same eyes as Ricky," I overheard Mark Dalton telling Wendy Summers whose response was

"Cummings?, he is waaay too young but if you shave off Mr. Jackson's mustache, he looks exactly like an older Ricky, I swear to God."

Walking around town you could sense a collective double take anytime a man in his early to mid-fifties would walk by. Everyone seemed to be thinking the same thoughts: Could *he* be? What if Ricky had plastic surgery? No wait how about him, or that guy, over by the phones oh good Lord, it's him. I know it, I just know it.

Those in the know had limited possible Rickys to several key suspects. There was Professor Louis Murdoch, who taught the popular *Cultural Impact of Pop Music in the 20th Century* class at the university. Professor Lou had been making the rounds of the talk show circuit and evidently knew way too much about Ricky Stevenson for some peoples taste. Not only was he approximately the right age, but the leather jacket he constantly wore reminded many of the one Ricky wore during his 1961 concert on the University Quad.

Then there was John Kelsey, proprietor of the Fotomat on Harrison Blvd. Mr. Kelsey was a painfully shy man with no discernible social life. Despite his quiet nature, Mr. Kelsey had a very handsome smile. His smile and hermit lifestyle had been enough to convince several of my friends, who were getting a lot more photos than usual developed lately.

I have even heard the name Dan Lewis batted around as a potential Ricky. I am pretty sure it's just because he is the only person in Delacourte other than Dad who has ever lived in L.A. and because of his love for 1950's and 60's design. If there is one person who doesn't look like Ricky

Stevenson it's Greg's father. I have seen black guys who look more like my father than Dan.

Basically any middle age fellow in our little town, who stood out in some way had been pinpointed as formerly being Ricky. The one person completely ignored in all the hoopla was Jack White. Dad had completely fallen under the radar lately, as it slips towards winter people tend to forget the storage industry even exists. Plus, my father raised blending in to an art. He still regularly went to all of his normal hangouts, including Hardware Express, Keller's Office Supply, Donut King, and Wilton's Sporting Goods. (Oh to be famous and get into all the hot spots.) To most residents of this little city Dad remained just Jack, that guy you make small talk with about heavy duty padlocks or glazed bearclaws. Friendly enough guy, owns some sort of business on the south end of town, I forgot what exactly.

You would think someone in this town would connect my resemblance to Ricky to my Dad, a fifty-something whose birthday just happens to be on August 22, the same day as Ricky Stevenson. I guess when you live in a town with a competitive university, and one of the largest concentrations of high I.Q.s in the Midwest you get a lot of clueless people. Thank goodness for this. If we did get found out I suspected my father would bail in a second and we would end up running another storage place in another boring little city. I would have to start over with no friends and a strange wardrobe, and I was used to my life here thank you very much.

•••

Friday, I made my usual pit stop at Wahl's Drugs before school in order to get my healthy Home Run Pie for breakfast and scan the tabloids for the newest Ricky news. As 8:00 grew ever closer I had to tear myself away from the thrilling headlines and head off to school. Once there I completely zoned off as usual. My day was spent fantasizing about Justine in a hot tub, doodling elaborate pictures of guitars, and having contests to see how long I could keep a pencil spinning, or standing up on its eraser. I also wondered endlessly about the auction that was taking place at one o'clock. If the auction was a public affair I would have skipped school in a second, but it is was open only to those select few who could afford to give a reasonable bid.

Rumors had been abounding about who the actual bidders will be. So far Jamie was the only bona fide celebrity to show up here in Delacourte, but there were reports of many other famous people showing interest in the Corvette. They either sent representatives here or wanted to bid by phone. The car was reportedly bid on by: two sheiks, an elusive member of English royalty, The Prince of Monaco, a representative for the Smithsonian museum, a casino magnate, a late night talk show host, the owner of a large chain of tire stores, and Ricky Stevenson's father. The final bid for my father's Corvette was supposed to set records. A Las Vegas casino even held bets for how much the final total would end up being.

You would think that this potential cash windfall would have been my Dad's main concern at the moment, but no. He somehow found the time to scream at me for two hours straight just because my grades have been slipping. Like it's any wonder, what with all that was going on.

The man was about to gain thousands, maybe millions of dollars for one of his possessions, his big secret was constantly in danger from all of the investigative reporters who have flooded our town, and his estranged father was been trying to claim the car for himself, but what did the artist formerly known as Ricky Stevenson choose to obsess over? One puny little insignificant C- on one little algebra test, that's what. The ever looming presence of Jack White had evidently kicked the ass and strangled the life out of Ricky several times over. No way was an insignificant little million dollar car auction going to revive our poor little rock god when there was a *mathematical exam* at stake.

I personally think I would do a hell of a lot better at algebra if the questions went something like this: Steven White has just sold his father's automobile or X for 3 million dollars. If the other members of his family: A, B, and C, want 0% of the money, but the IRS wants 20% of the profits from X, how much money does Steven receive from the sale of the automobile? This is a problem that is definitely worth pulling out the old calculator for--hell I would even do this problem with a slide rule if I had to.

Chapter 34
One Hell of a Nest Egg

For 1.2 million dollars Jamie Underwood got to remain in the limelight a little longer or maybe a lot longer. His smile was all over the news after he turned in the winning bid. If I wasn't mistaken it looked a little more genuine, than it did to me when I first saw him get off the plane in Indianapolis. Jamie was constantly repeating his mantra about how Ricky would have wanted the car to go to someone he knew, and he announced that he will allow a car museum to tour it around the country next summer.

Jeanne and I each got a fourth of the profits to help pay for college and a house when we get old enough.

"Or a down payment on a one bedroom condo if you are really planning to move to L.A., Steven," Dad joked.

Until graduation from college, Jeanne and I couldn't go anywhere near these accounts. I wondered if my father would count an Associate's Degree from Dexter Community College as good enough to claim my money. I decided it would be better to bring it up later.

The remaining portion of the money was going toward a possible expansion of the Stor'N'More, a replacement for the station wagon, new furniture, and nicer vacations for the four of us. All of the new purchases would be done very slowly, so we didn't alert any of our fellow townsfolk. It was best if no one noticed the Whites had somehow mysteriously joined the ranks of the nouveau riche.

We didn't know how much money we would eventually end up with until the tax service Stan Johnson recommended came up with a final estimate. They were busy setting up bank accounts and stocks, bonds and money market funds for us, and I had a distinct feeling that a good percentage of the proceeds would ensure that our little secret remained a secret.

...

Once the car sold, Delacourte finally started to return to normal. The teeming masses had abruptly left leaving piles of unsold Ricky Stevenson T-shirts and other memorabilia in their wake. Downtown once again looked deserted, and the giant posters of Ricky were taken down to be auctioned off to benefit the elementary school's music program. Needless to say they were not expecting 1.2 million dollars.

All of the respected members of the press had left as well, headed towards the Middle East where the president was having yet another round of peace talks, or to Florida where there have been several small floods. Some of the tabloid reporters lingered on, probably searching for Ricky's mystery woman, but they kept coming up short. In time they would also leave. Some celebrity or politician somewhere was bound to have a sex scandal of some sort. The country was quite overdue, there had not been one in three or four months.

Most of the popular crowd already forgot about their temporary case of Ricky-itis and were embracing a rap song about a character from an upcoming horror movie. The Ricky Stevenson fanclub now only consisted of me, my friends and a Japanese foreign exchange student obsessed with the fifties. I went back to ignoring the popular people and vice versa.

I had been angry with them even before the car was sold. Sure it was fantastic when I got invited to three popular parties in one week, but then Dan Parker asked me if I had most of the songs down pat.

"Songs?" I asked him.

"Yeah dude--aren't you playing Ricky Stevenson songs at Mark Jackson's party?"

"Oh yeah something's come up. I don't know if I can make it," I told him. That was the moment I had realized I was just a novelty to the popular people, someone to laugh at until something else came along to amuse them. Forget that, I was through trying to impress the popular crowd. My new mantra was: let people come and try to impress me. You want to be my friend, you have to earn it. I am going for quality, not quantity. Maybe my father's experience was rubbing off on me after all. Who knew?

...

I was even able to once again concentrate on school a bit more, just before we were off for Thanksgiving break. It was obvious that I was never destined to be able to sustain my scholarly concentration skills for more than two weeks at a time.

Our family usually has Thanksgiving with my mother's parents, but this year Grandma and Grandpa were going on a cruise to Mexico. Mom's brother and sister live far enough from us that they also decided it was not worth making the trip for just a couple of days. The four of us were on our own.

It was reassuring to not have to deal with any relatives for once. I mean I love my extended family and all, but they always force me from my comfortable bed onto an uncomfortable couch. Every holiday at least one of them would wake me up at some crazy hour because they couldn't remember where the bathroom is.

When they did eventually visit, it was going to be weird not being able to talk about what was going on in our lives. We can't mention the car, or how it turns out that guess what: my pop's actually famous rock'n'roller who everyone thinks is dead. Isn't that amazing huh Grandpa? Or to translate for the older generation--think of it like waking up one day and finding out that your dad is Benny Goodman, but please don't tell anyone okay. I mean you guys don't want to shock your canasta pals with the story of how your daughter was seduced by a swaying, hip gyrating hooligan do you?

Hopefully by the time Christmas rolled around Jeanne and I would be completely used to pretending nothing's going on, so we could easily deal with Grandma, Grandpa, Aunt Sally and Uncle Mike, Uncle Dan and Aunt Rene, Great Aunt Erma, various screaming cousins and whatever other relatives felt the need to stop by. It had been hard enough keeping this secret from my friends, but to not be able to talk to the relatives was going be a much more intense test of my resolve.

Grandma and Grandpa would be the hardest to keep mum around. A visit with them always entailed the grilling of Jeanne and me about the intimate details of our lives. Every breakfast with them was a litany of:

"So Steven, got yourself a girlfriend yet?" or

"Steven your mother tells us you have taken up the guitar. You have got to play something for us, you know your grandfather used to play the ukulele. You don't happen to know that song *Yes We Have No Bananas* do you? I used to love that song."

Then there was my cousin Amy, who was the closest to my age and had a talent for drawing secrets from people. Amy would talk about her latest boyfriend for what seemed like hours on end, before abruptly stopping, and turning the conversation over to what was happening in my life.

"Come on Steve, you have to tell me what's going on in your life. Don't be shy," Amy would ask, and I always told her.

She not only knew that I had a never ending crush on a certain girl, but she knew Justine's name, hair color, and favorite perfume. I think I always shared too much with Amy because she shared too much with me. I don't think it ever occurred to Amy that I had no need to know about how Dan Myerson had dumped her behind the roller rink, (that bastard!) or how Reggie Pearson made the absolute best mix tapes for all of his girlfriends. (I gotta admit Reggie's summer of '92 mix is pretty epic.)

I had the feeling that whenever the relatives stopped by, be it at Christmas, or sometime afterward, I was going to spend a lot of time in my room or behind the storage spaces ignoring everyone. There had to be a trick to dealing with the family secret. I walked upstairs in search of expert advice.

"So what did you want to talk to me about, Steven?" Mom asked, after I had located her folding laundry in front of the TV in the master bedroom.

Was it ever hard for you knowing Dad's secret, and keeping it from everybody?" I asked.

"Oh God yes," she told me. "By the mid-seventies Ricky's story had sort of faded into the background, but then that movie *Rock and Roll Runaway* came out in 1977. Suddenly the entire country was fixated on Ricky Stevenson again. Everywhere I looked there would be images of Ricky on posters, notebooks, even lunchboxes. There was no avoiding it. I was pregnant with you at the time, so I was having a lot of crazy emotions anyway, then I would be at the grocery store and suddenly there would be a young version of my husband peering out from the magazine rack," My mother paused a second and grabbed another shirt from the laundry basket.

"Jack didn't look anything like Ricky at the time," she continued. "He still had that awful beard, but no matter what he did, your father could never hide the fact that he still had

Ricky's smile, and those famous blue eyes. I would be in the magazine aisle of the store and all I could think was: I am about to have that man's baby, Ricky Stevenson's about to become a father and I can't tell a soul. It was very surreal. I am the only person in the world who has sat next to Ricky Stevenson in a darkened movie theater, while carrying his child, and watched a movie about his life and disappearance," Mom smiled at this memory.

"Anyway," She continued. "Elvis died later that year so all the attention drifted to him. Once I gave birth to you and Jeanne all that mattered to me was being a parent. I didn't pay much attention to pop culture unless it was *Sesame Street*, and as the years passed, Jack would look less and less like Ricky, so it was much easier to think of them as two separate people. I didn't even mind it when he started asking me to buy various Ricky Stevenson books and magazines for his collection inside seventeen.

I scarcely remembered the feelings I once had until you got older and began to look so much like your father," Mom was looking directly at me now. The iron sat unused. "Then came your decision to be Ricky Stevenson for Halloween that one year," she said. "I thought your poor father was going to have a heart attack, but eventually we both got used to your endless fascination with the man he once was. It's gotten so I can hardly remember what you look like without all of that mousse in your hair."

...

The next day as I sat at the dining room table devouring Mom's moist turkey and Jeanne's burnt stuffing, I looked around at our much smaller than usual Thanksgiving crowd and began to wonder if there might be relatives we have never met on my father's side of the family. The story Jeanne and I had always been told was that Dad's mom died when he was very young and he had a fight with his father, who had later moved out of the country and we didn't know what happened to him.

Now, we know the truth about Bob Stevenson. (Who I couldn't bring myself to think of as anything other than Robert or Bob Stevenson--*definitely not* Grandpa, although technically he is.) As for any other relatives, there apparently are not many. Dad was an only child, and his mother died when he was nine. After he disappeared a few distant cousins came out of the woodwork, but they promptly vanished once they found out they were not getting anything.

Jeanne and I never thought much about Dad's side of the family. The plethora of relatives from Mom's side more than made up for it. We always had plenty of aunts, uncles, grandparents, and cousins around when we needed them.

...

The day after Thanksgiving we had all had our fill of leftover turkey and football so my father grabbed the remote and started flipping, stopping on some news program's story about Ricky Stevenson. Since the hype around the car had faded there were a lot less Ricky related stories, but still more than usual. This one was a fluff piece all about Bob Stevenson and his anguish about not knowing if his son was alive. My father wasn't talking back to the TV like he usually did when watching a Ricky related item. Instead he kept shifting his legs and grimacing as the reporter asked Bob cheesy questions like:

"Do you think there is a chance, Ricky could still be alive after all these years?" and "if you could see your son, what would you say to him?"

Bob gave tear filled answers like, "I don't know but I pray every single day just for one chance," and "I would just tell him I am sorry, let's start over," in between shots of him walking in front of several childhood photos of Ricky, while syrupy music played in the background. The segment wrapped up when the reporter faced the camera directly and said, "For now it looks like Bob's questions will go unanswered, as hard as it has been dealing with the mysterious disappearance of his son, it's even harder to live with the cancer slowly spreading in his lungs. This Thanksgiving as many gather with their families Robert Stevenson only has the memories of his missing son."

"Oh lord, is he still an actor," Dad said, after hitting mute when the television switched to a commercial break.

"Maybe it's time to make peace with him," my mother said to him.

"Why doesn't he go on TV and say he's sorry for what he did to her, and me. The man knows exactly why he drove me away," Dad responded.

"What did he do?" Jeanne asked.

I could tell Dad didn't want to answer her because he took his time before answering.

"He smacked me around some, but I guess everyone did back then. I could take it but my mom never deserved it. She was ailing already. That's why I never forgave him. You don't hit a woman, let alone a sick woman."

The room stayed still for a couple of minutes until Dad spoke again.

"I can't leave it like this. I always thought I could, but I am a better man than that. I don't want to have regrets. I know dad's got plenty of them whether he wants to admit or not. I guess we have to go."

That's why we decided to head to Los Angeles during our Christmas break. Not so I can tour colleges, or so Jeanne can see Disneyland, but so my father can make peace with the old man who used to beat him and the young man he used to be.

Chapter 35
Royal Fester Terrace

Los Angeles, California

I had never seen so many apartments in my entire life. These were not the tall brick apartments with awnings and doormen you see on TV shows, but boring two and three story buildings that all seem to have been built circa 1965. Each one had a cheesy name like *The Tahitian* or *The Royale*, and the only thing separating one block of apartments from the next was a strip mall on the corner. Even the shopping centers here looked exactly the same. They all contained a Mexican chicken place, a Laundromat, and a liquor store with a sign half in English and half in Spanish or Korean or Farsi.

I am pretty sure my father's grand plan was to get me to hate Los Angeles with such a grand passion that I would never ever want to give up the glamour and excitement of helping others load their old appliances into storage lockers. So far the plan was working out very well.

We had been driving through apartmentopia for at least three hours because there was no way in hell my father would ever admit he had gotten lost in the area where he grew up. As soon as we got our bags from the airport carousel and rented a convertible my father drove directly to a Holiday Inn. Now, the average person who suddenly comes into a lot of money and heads to Los Angeles would live it up at the Beverly Hills Hotel, but in case you haven't noticed my family about as far from normal as you can get. Sadly, it seems the Whites are never destined to have mints on our pillows and terrycloth robes provided for us. Oh well, at least it was a cool Holiday Inn. I never stayed in a round hotel before.

After we dropped the bags off in our room, Dad asked us if we wanted to drive around. Partially circular or not, there is nothing in the world more boring than a hotel room, so we agreed mistakenly thinking he would drive us to somewhere typical tourists go like Hollywood, or the beach at sunset. Instead Dad headed north, got off the freeway and promptly got us lost in this maze of dense lower middle class housing. Along the way, our happy conversation went something like this:

"I've got jet lag. Can we go back to the hotel now?"

"In a minute. Everything's gone, I can't believe it. They have paved over my entire childhood."

"I'm starving. When are we going to eat?"

"Do you see any restaurants?"

"Jack where exactly are we heading? I'm getting a little hungry as well."

"Would you just give me ONE SECOND to find my bearings It's been thirty years for chrissakes."

"Maybe we should just stop to ask for directions."

"I don't need to stop for directions. I just need to find Sepulveda. Once I find Sepulveda I can find the freeway again, no problem."

"Look, there's an IHOP. Can we get some food-- please?"

"We didn't just fly 2000 miles to eat at a damn IHOP."

"Then how about that place over there Pol-lo Grande."

"Poy-Yo Grand-Ay. God, it's no wonder you get such bad grades."

"Sorry the sign says Pol-lo besides I don't take Spanish I take French, so what the heck is a Poy-Yo anyway?"

"It's chicken. Now would you please shut up and let me drive. Dammit he just cut me off!"

Once we eventually found Sepulveda Boulevard, did my father use that opportunity to hop on the freeway like he promised? No of course not. Instead we drove down Sepulveda for what seemed like ages passing more crappy apartments, scary looking markets, used car lots, and junky motels until he finally turned and started navigating random side streets again.

After what seemed like an eternity, the car came to an abrupt halt. I jerked open my eyes which I had shut in a desperate effort to pretend we were driving through the mansions of Beverly Hills.

"Well here it is, just as ugly as I remember," Dad said pointing at one of the buildings.

I looked up where he was pointing, on the outset it looked like we were in front of yet another rundown apartment building smack dab in the middle of Van Nuys, California, but then I spotted a street sign that read: Kester Ave. Within a matter of seconds I knew that we were at a hallowed place many Rock and Roll fans dream of making a pilgrimage to, the childhood home of Ricky Stevenson.

The apartment consisted of a pair of two story buildings with an ancient swimming pool in a courtyard between them. Each building had a faded mustard and olive green color scheme. On the front of one of the buildings you could barely make out the name *Royal Kester Terrace* painted in swirly sixties style letters alongside a logo of a palm tree. To say that the experience was underwhelming was the understatement of the year.

Rumor is Bob Stevenson is still the owner of the Royal Kester Terrace, and has deliberately done nothing with the building. While other people might rename the place Stevenson Arms, add some murals of Ricky, along with a museum and a gift shop, Bob Stevenson has done nothing with the place. He must be ashamed of Ricky's childhood home, and his former role as owner and manager. I guess

Bob figures you have to be a diehard Ricky fan to deliberately seek this dump out from all the similar apartments in the area.

"Damn Royal Fester Terrace. Still a pit," my father muttered as he started the car and we headed off.

We ended up eating dinner at the Holiday Inn's restaurant then we headed up to our room. The jet lag was really starting to set in so we decide to leave the Los Angeles nightlife for another time. I grabbed the TV remote and started flipping until I landed on one of the local stations. They were showing *Bikini Beach Barbecue*.

"There is no way in hell we are watching that," Dad told me.

"I've already seen it," I responded.

"Well I hope it didn't scar you too badly," he said, as he made me hand over the remote.

Chapter 36
Sightseeing

Dad's plan now involved putting off confronting his father for as long as possible, not that I could blame him. It wasn't like we could all drive up to the Bel Air mansion of Bob Stevenson, knock on the door and say:

"Hey what's up? Remember me?"

With all the hoopla from the car sale, and the TV interview the area around Bob's house had become a smaller version of the circus that surrounded Delacourte. We drove by one morning just to see the place from the outside, but all we saw was a large wrought iron gate. Several people mingled about while a security officer repeatedly tried unsuccessfully to shoo them away.

The morning was pretty warm, especially to those of us used to Midwest winters, but Dad insisted that we keep the convertible's top up as we drove through the streets of Bel Air. Everywhere we turned were massive homes that could have been ours had my father not ran away that day in '64. A thick air of unspoken tension was wafted through the car, the bulk of which emanated from the driver's seat. The closer we got to the house the stronger it became. If it was this bad now, how was it going to be when we finally confronted Bob Stevenson?

Dad finally spoke as we stopped at the intersection just past the house.

"Oh God what if these people recognized me? This was a really bad idea Ellen," He said. "Half of them probably work for the tabloids. No one saw them snap any pictures of us did you?"

"Relax Jack," my mother did her best to reassure him. "Those people looked like ordinary tourists to me, same as us. We are just an ordinary family from Indiana in what is obviously a rental car, and you look nothing like Ricky anymore. You know that. Please don't be paranoid."

"Okay, maybe I don't look much like I used to but I am still the same person aren't I? There has to be some resemblance. They must be expecting a middle aged man," he said. "What if they see Steven? He looks exactly like the Ricky everybody remembers. Steven are you wearing that hat?" He gave a quick glance towards the back seat.

I quickly put on the tacky blue cap with Los Angeles embroidered on it in sparkly thread that Dad had bought me in the hotel's gift shop. I usually hate caps, as they mess with the usual gelled--with just a touch of old man pomade--look of my hair, but I was not about to bring up that particular point.

"Let's just go get some breakfast, I think we will all feel better once we have some food," Mom said as she tried to ignore the jerkiness of the car as Dad maneuvered down the hill as quickly as he could.

My father's driving had taken on a new personality since we arrived in Los Angeles. Maybe it was the rented convertible, which we got as part of a "California Sunshine Special" through the auto club, or the fact that he still believed he knew the place like the back of his hand, when he clearly didn't. Maybe Dad was simply slipping back into the reckless teenager with too much money and a fast car mode. I suspected young, cocky millionaire Ricky Stevenson had a tendency to be hell on wheels. Whatever the cause, I was sure Dad's uncertain command of the rental car was going to give my poor mother a heart attack. She kept tensing up, jerking her head around, and generally acting the way she does when I am the one behind the wheel.

We ended up at a very ordinary coffee shop but nobody complained out of fear we would set Dad off completely. Once our plates arrived; filled with pancakes, sausages, eggs, and bacon, the tension quickly began to melt. Finally it was replaced by a large sigh from my father.

"I feel so much better. I guess I was just hungry. Richard is starting to come back but I can definitely deal with him on a full stomach."

"Richard?" Jeanne asked out loud exactly what I was thinking.

"You know who I mean. Ricky," He said the name in a whisper, while glancing side to side.

"How did you get Ricky from Richard anyway?" Jeanne asked ignoring Dad's hiss.

"For one thing my father gave me the name Richard, and for another I always loathed the names Richie or Dick."

At the mention of the name Dick I stifled a laugh. I heard a snort and noticed Jeanne was making a desperate effort to keep her orange juice down.

After we paid the tab and stepped outside Dad said, "let's go to the beach," as he started putting down the convertible's top.

So we all piled in, knowing the promise of finally seeing the Pacific in all its glory was finally about to happen.

Dad found his bearings a lot more easily than he had the previous day, and within moments we turned onto Sunset. At the first intersection he turned the radio down.

"This is great," he announced. "I can drive down Sunset in a convertible with my girl by my side and no one notices me in the least. I should have done this, years ago. Look there's *The Whisky a Go Go*. I played there a couple of times. The last time Jamie had so much to drink he passed out and ended up at Cedars."

He pointed out a few more landmarks then announced:

"Let's see the house. No trip to Los Angeles is complete without a trip to Ricky Stevenson's house, and besides I know the back way."

I quickly braced myself for a repeat of the morning. I figured we would end up a couple of blocks from the house, where my father would see a throng of fans and immediately turn us around. Just in case we got reasonably close, I put on the hat and my sunglasses, and checked my new Mr. Average look in Jeanne's compact mirror. I forgot just how much of a complete geek I look like with a hat on. Oh well.

Much to my surprise, Dad made it all the way up Oceanside Avenue, and we ended up parking four houses away. Despite the fact that a tour bus was slowly making its way past the house; it wasn't nearly as crowded as I expected. Aside from those who were seated on the bus, only a few clumps of people were mingling about. They looked like they were trying to hide their obvious disappointment. All you could see of Ricky's Stevenson's former residence was a pepto bismol colored rooftop peeking from behind a tall wood gate awash in ivy, and numerous security protection signs.

I knew all of the people mingling about had to be tourists because they sported the type of outfits you can only get away with wearing when you are on vacation. It was a sea of ugly sandals worn with clashing socks, fanny packs, and T-shirts from every over-priced chain restaurant in existence. I even saw a cap identical to mine perched on a man who didn't have the toned and fit physique that L.A. residents all supposedly had. This man's girth was pure mid-America in all of its glory, for all I know he could have been from Delacourte.

Dad walked up to the gate ignoring the signs and tried to find a knothole by pushing some of the ivy to the side.

"Can't see a damn thing," he announced. "Okay let's go."

As we drove away from the house he said, "I certainly don't blame whoever lives there for replacing my gate with that huge one. It must be such a pain to have throngs of strangers mingling about all the time."

"You mean like the customers who are always mingling around our house, trying to get past our gate?" I asked him.

"Ha ha, that's completely different and you know it. Anyway if you guys ever want to see what it looked like when I lived there, I have a copy of the *Western Architecture* featuring it in one of my bins."

...

The beach turned out to be somewhat of a disappointment because it was way too cold to swim and there was hardly anyone around. Jeanne and I ripped off our socks and shoes then headed toward the water just so we could be able to say we had been in the Pacific Ocean. Two seconds later we were both in complete agony from the icy water lapping at our all too vulnerable toes. I was quite sure that pneumonia would set in at any moment.

A few surfers were braving the frigid waters, even though there were hardly any waves. Those slick black wetsuits must be a lot warmer than they looked. A few other tourists were taking photos in front of the ocean and the empty lifeguard station. We got our obligatory shots in as well, and since there were no decent shells to be found, I grabbed a couple of the nicer looking rocks to keep.

After our stop at the beach, we headed over to Hollywood where we did the usual sightseeing. We saw the Chinese and Egyptian Theaters, and Mom muttered her disgust about the sheer number of adult stores located nearby. My father tried to locate his star on the walk of fame, but somehow he had completely forgotten its location.

"How the heck can you not remember where your star is?" I asked him, mystified. "I mean didn't they give you a little plaque and a location map when you got it?"

"They gave it to me after I disappeared. Did you know you have to purchase these things? Emcee Records was too cheap to buy me one when I was around, but as soon as I was gone they saw it as an opportunity to keep Ricky in the public eye. Hell they paid so much that the committee bent its rules about having the star's recipient present at the ceremony. Though I suspect they were secretly hoping I would put in an appearance anyway."

"It's just as well," Mom piped in. "It's probably smack dab in front of one of these filthy stores and I don't want Steven looking in any of the windows of those places."

Judging from my mother's rather naive viewpoint, I suspected she had never found the secret stash of magazines Joey gave me for my fifteenth birthday that I kept hidden beneath my videotape collection in my footlocker. It was good to know I had a mom who respected my privacy. According to my friends, a mother who didn't ransack their kid's room on a daily basis was a blessing indeed.

After we got tired of looking at other celebrities' stars we ended up inside a wax museum. If I'm not mistaken wax Ricky's eyes had a trapped animal longing to flee quality to them. This was probably because the museum people had wax Ricky facing a doorway with a neon question mark glowing over it. He was holding a suitcase in one hand, and a guitar case in the other.

...

"Can we go to Disneyland tomorrow?" Jeanne asked, as we got ready for bed that night.

"Sure why not?" my father said. "You know one of the best concerts I ever had was at Disneyland."

"I've never heard of a Ricky Stevenson Concert at Disneyland," I told him.

"That's because I wasn't famous yet. I was still just another local Southern California kid with a band, and Jamie knew a guy who worked on the Jungle Cruise who somehow got us a gig there. Anyway it was a great concert; we were just these regular kids playing our hearts out, and not caring if anybody was listening or not. Suddenly all these kids came and started dancing to our music. They could have chosen to go on the rides but instead they decided to listen to us. I would have chosen the rides myself, but I guess that's because I was a pretty bad dancer. Afterward we hung out with a few of the kids in the audience and really saw the place. It was one of the first times I had ever gotten a real response from an audience, and it was fantastic. It was my first taste of the upside of fame and I was so naive back then, I didn't realize that there was a downside as well.

Now if you ask any of the other Sleepers what our best concert was they will probably mention The Hollywood Bowl, or the time we played The Cow Palace. These were both great concerts, but my answer remains that one evening at Disneyland. Knowing this, is it any wonder that I was never cut out to be famous?"

Dad paused for a few minutes then said, "Sometimes I really miss playing. It was one of the only parts of being Ricky I liked. Whether it was in the studio or up on stage, I used to love the times when I could just get lost in a song. Sure, there were the days when I couldn't get going and I wanted to go home, but then there were the times when the guys and I could have jammed forever. I was happy on stage making people forget their troubles for a little while, and getting them to sing along and dance," Dad stretched himself on the hotel bed. It groaned, of course.

"Thank God for the outlets I installed in seventeen," he continued. "I used to occasionally get the old urge so I would head over to the space in the middle of the night and play my old songs. I was always worried I would wake up you kids, but I must have insulated the walls pretty well because you never did.

Of course once Steven got himself a guitar I didn't have to play in the middle of the night anymore. I probably shouldn't admit this but that little guitar has gotten me through many a slow day at the Stor'N'More, while you guys were at work or school. She's actually not a bad little instrument."

"Why do guys always think cars and guitars are girls anyway?" Jeanne interrupted. "I am going to learn guitar and mine is going to be a man. His name is going to be Joe or Ralph and I won't let any men or boys play with him ever. I won't let them drive my car Dan, either."

The next day at Disneyland I saw a Beatles tribute band play on a stage in Tomorrowland. Even though the stage was tiny, and our family was the only one watching the show, when that stage came out of the ground I found myself wanting to be on the stage, playing my guitar and making people dance.

Chapter 37
Jack Makes the Call

As our trip wound down, we were starting to get tired of Los Angeles, but Dad kept putting off the one thing we had come here to take care of. We were done visiting the beach, Disneyland, Universal Studios, Hollywood, and every other typical Southern California tourist attraction.

I was even beginning to miss the snow. I hate shoveling, walking on slippery ice and the bitter cold, as much as anybody, but it just didn't feel like the holiday season around here. The weather was warm and ugly, the bright blue skies that greeted us the first couple of days, were replaced by an ugly haze that settled over everything and burned our eyes. The only seasonal reminders we saw were tinsel decorations on palm trees, banners attached to light poles, and store windows painted with snowflakes, reindeer, and Santas.

Christmas fell early during the break and we spent a somewhat uneventful one back home in Delacourte. None of our relatives had stopped by because they figured it wasn't worth the effort since our flight was on the 27th. My presents were typical assortment of stuff I had asked for; like my new portable CD player, and things I didn't, like a bag of socks with the K-mart pricetag still attached.

Jeanne got me a scale model of a '59 Corvette and another Ricky Stevenson action figure (okay okay, doll). This Ricky was not in an unopened package. Instead Jeanne had replaced his original clothes with a miniature flannel shirt and jeans combo, which she possibly stolen from Mattel's *Village People* Ken. (Model #4 construction worker) Jeanne had him holding a tiny paper cube which was made to look like a cardboard box. She called this gift the Stor'N'More Ricky.

As we drove around aimlessly looking for something to do, Jeanne suggested visiting Panorama City. Dad gave her a look that said: are you completely insane?

"Why do you want to go there?" He asked.

"Didn't you stay with some guy there once? Remember, you told us about it the night we went to the nasty salmon place back home," she said.

"That was just something I told you kids when I didn't want you to know I used to live here." he responded. "Anyway we drove through there the other day. Right after I showed you my old apartment."

"That was Panorama city?" Jeanne asked.

"Yes," Dad said.

"I don't remember seeing any views. What are the panoramas of? I thought it was going to be, like a canyon or something." Jeanne was evidently not impressed with the naming skills of San Fernando Valley's pioneers.

"The only panoramic views it has nowadays are of tacky houses and used car dealerships," Dad told her.

...

Mom was getting tired of all the traffic and kept losing her patience with Dad. My father continually got us lost on freeways that had not been built when he last lived here. Apparently in the 1950's and 60's all of the area freeways were named for destinations, but over time they have been expanded so much they all go by numbers now. This drove

Dad completely insane. As we drove in circles on the same freeway we had gotten lost on the day before, he and Mom would argue. All of their arguments sounded like this.

"Now wait if the five is the Golden State, then what the hell is the Santa Ana? I thought Santa Ana was the five. Just where the hell does this Golden State go?"

"I don't know Jack, but it looks like you were in the wrong lane on the interchange. According to the sign we are now headed for someplace called Simi Valley."

"Simi Valley? Simi Valley doesn't have a freeway? It's in the middle of nowhere. Are you sure that's what the sign said?"

"Yes that's what the sign said. At any rate this sure looks like it goes somewhere to me."

Mom finally faked a bout with food poisoning to get my father to stop at a gas station. When she got back from "the restroom" her arms were full of maps covering every part of Southern California. Dad grumbled something about a useless expense and wasting money, before he consulted the maps, just to verify he was already right.

Dad's trips down memory lane were also starting to grate on the rest of us as we drove through miles and miles of seedy looking used car lots and rundown houses only to find that whatever he was looking for had been replaced by a laundromat. According to Dad, when he was young; all of the car parts stores, pawn shops, and sleazy adult bookstores we passed were either orange groves or farmland. I shut my eyes and tried to imagine this but I just couldn't. I was sure Dad had to be exaggerating. This must be the California equivalent to stories of spending your childhood walking to school uphill ten miles in the snow.

Dad was especially distressed that there were hardly any Bob's Big Boy restaurants left. We would drive for miles and miles only to find out that another one of his childhood burger stands was now a Denny's or a carwash. I didn't know why the heck he was so upset. We used to eat at a Big Boy all the time on our way to Uncle Dan's house in

Chicago, and he didn't seem overly broken up when that one closed.

...

Our winter break was coming to an end, and Mom and Dad didn't want Jeanne and I to miss any school. Confronting Bob Stevenson was the only thing we had left to do, and I had the feeling this was going to be a major hassle. Dad kept picking up the receiver of hotel room's phone then putting it down before he actually made the call. I suspected Dad would not be the first person to call up Bob Stevenson claiming to be his long lost son. Mom must have had the same idea since she turned to him and said.

"Why don't you have Stan Johnson call him and arrange this."

Stan Johnson was evidently the cure-all when it came to our Ricky related crises. I wondered if he was the sole link between my father's past and current identity. Could there have been others outside our family who knew of both? I wondered why the mysterious Stan had stayed so loyal. Had my father once saved his life, paid him off substantially, or was there something more?

I also wondered what Stan thought the night the car was moved from the Stor'N'More to the University Gym. Did he nearly go into cardiac arrest over the fact that *Ricky Stevenson* was now the owner of a Midwestern storage rental place, or was it along the lines of what he was expecting? Did Stan like my mother? Did he know about Jeanne and me? Would we ever meet him? I asked Dad about Stan a few times but his answers were always vague.

Dad mulled over my mother's suggestion to get Stan in contact with Robert Stevenson. He shifted his weight on the sagging motel bed, then turned to her and said.

"Stan's done way to much already. I guess I'll call dad myself. This number is supposed to be pretty direct. Maybe I'll get dad himself on the line."

He reached over and picked up the phone. Jeanne and I eavesdropped while pretending to watch some cartoons playing on the room's TV. Dad didn't buy our little act.

"Why the heck are you guys watching cartoons? You are both teenagers for god's sake," he snapped.

We abruptly shut the TV off, and stopped hiding our obvious interest in the impending conversation. Dad mumbled a few muffled curses as he tried to navigate the hotels operator system until he finally got through.

"Hello Bob Stevenson please," Dad's voice sounded peeved that the number Stan provided had not gained him direct access to our elusive paternal grandfather.

"Jeffery Harrison, I knew his son in High School, and I used to help maintain the apartment's pool back in the fifties."

"Tell him I have something of Ricky's he would be very interested in."

"Look its personal, why don't you tell Bob, that if he doesn't let me through, he will regret it for the rest of his life."

"It's not Jeffery, I just used his name to get past your secretary, it's me, Ricky."

"Look, I know a lot of people have called you in the past pretending to be me, but ask me something only Ricky would know."

At that precise moment my father gave a sharp look to my mother, who in turn gave us another sharp look in response, and we somehow found ourselves out in the hall. I was dying to know what that one thing only Ricky would know was, but she shut the door before I could overhear.

"Come on kids," Mom said. Your father needs some time to talk lets go for a walk."

We navigated our way around the round hallways of the hotel until we ended up at the pool, where we sat on some chaise lounges for a few minutes absorbing the eye watering chlorine fumes emanating from the water.

Jeanne turned to Mom and asked.

"So is Dad gonna meet his father somewhere or are they just going to talk on the phone?

"I assume your father would want to talk face to face, especially since we are here in LA., I guess it's up to Bob though," Mom responded.

"Are we coming with Dad, or is this something he wants to do alone?" I asked, secretly hoping for the latter answer.

"I discussed it with your father, and if Bob wants to meet we are all going to go. I think you should at least meet your grandfather. Even though he has done some bad things in the past, Bob's probably just a sick old man who deserves a second chance," Mom said.

"Yeah but a rich sick old man, who I don't want to meet. I don't want to know anybody who would ever hit a woman. It's no wonder Dad left." Jeanne piped in. "He's probably gonna have reporters at his house who are going to rat us out."

"We probably won't end up at his Bel Air house, not with all those people perched outside. According to Stan he has a ranch near Ventura, where stays a lot. We will probably meet him near there."

Chapter 38
Robert Stevenson

As it turned out Bob Stevenson did want to meet us all in Ventura. I thought we were going to end up at his ranch but instead we ended up at a generic looking seafood restaurant. I guess this was somewhat appropriate seeing as how my grandfather had the same name as the guy who wrote *Treasure Island.* (Though I doubt his middle name is Louis, I think I read somewhere that it's Henry.) We sat uncomfortably waiting at our table looking at the stuff posted on the dark oak walls like pilot's wheels, netting, and stuffed marlins, while we scanned the almost empty restaurant for his arrival.

If Dad was upset or worried that the meeting was taking place in a public he didn't show it. He was eerily calm. On the other hand, I was seriously worried Bob would show up with a camera crew from *Fame Daily* or at least have several tabloid reporters planted throughout the restaurant. I glanced up at the walls again. Could there be a hidden camera inside that spyglass? A tape recorder hidden behind that anchor? Could that old lady being seated--really be a tabloid reporter in drag?

Much to my relief Bob showed up alone several minutes later. He looked a lot frailer than he did on television, and was shuffling along with the help of a metal cane. Dad probably thought the cane was all part of an act, and was surprised Bob hadn't brought along an oxygen tank, and a blonde nurse named Tammy who's breasts would look like they had been recently filled by said oxygen tank.

"Good God you have let yourself go Richard." were the first loving words to spill from my grandfather's mouth. "I would never have recognized you in a million years if it wasn't for him" he said and nodded his head towards me. The now omnipresent tacky blue cap didn't hide my Ricky-esque looks as much as I previously thought, so I took it off.

My father kept his voice cold and said. "Well people get do older and I am no exception. It's seems neither are you."

"All right I didn't come here to argue, do any of them have names?"

Them evidently meant us since my father went through a quick introduction. "This is Ellen, this is Jeanne, and this is Steven."

"Hello nice to meet you all, please forgive me for acting cold earlier, I have no problem with any of you just Richard, or whatever his name is now."

"You can call me Richard."

"Fine, so Richard, where exactly have you been the past thirty years anyway?"

"We live in the Midwest."

"The Midwest huh, well that really narrows it down doesn't it? Let me guess you guys live near that town where they sold the Corvette. What's it called Decatur, Declure? Well whatever. If I need to find out, I'll find out."

"Why should I tell you anything dad," My father locked his eyes with Bob's. It was eerie how they both had eyes in the exact shade of deep blue. "As I recall you tried to take the car for yourself. That's not particularly trustworthy behavior in my opinion. Or am I supposed to believe you're hurting for cash?"

"I didn't want the car, that was all my lawyers' idea," Robert said. "It takes a whole slew of them to make sure they don't put the Ricky Stevenson image on toilet seat covers and Japanese beer. Protecting the trademark is what they call it. Emptying my wallet is what I call it. Anyway I went along because I just wanted to know if you were alive. Now I know, and I'm satisfied. I didn't come here with a bunch of reporters, and I don't have any spies for the WorldWide News posted as waiters or anything. You don't have to believe me but I've stayed true to my word."

Just then our real waiter showed up, causing Bob to abruptly cut his conversation short. Since the waiter was about my age, with a bad case of acne, I seriously doubted he could be a spy for any sort of a tabloid, but who knows.

Once the waiter left after serving us with a plate full of cheese biscuits and our drinks my father spoke.

"Look Dad, I had a lot of reasons for doing what I did. Believe it or not you were only a small factor in my decision. We never got along that well, and had I stayed around I seriously doubt we would have ever been close. Truth is I don't even know why I came here, but I did. You and I both know this is probably the last time we will ever see each other, so we can make the effort worthwhile, or we can continue to argue." Dad paused for a second to try one of the cheese biscuits.

"I've read plenty of your interviews where you go on and on about how you've found God, you've realized you were wrong, and you would do anything for just one more chance," he continued. "Well looky here, you gained that magical chance and what do you do? Within two seconds you prove that the whole forgiveness bit is just a big act."

The waiter came back with our fish and Jeanne's hamburger. Dad and Bob each made their eyes into eerily similar slits, while my mother looked nervously towards Jeanne who was staring out the window at the harbor. After the waiter left we silently chewed our food a few minutes until Bob spoke.

"Mmmm, there's nothing I love more than I good pile of popcorn shrimp. Of course my doctor doesn't want me to eat anything fried but I mostly ignore his advice anyway. That may explain all the ulcers. You there, Jeanne is it? My wife's name was Jeanne did you know that? Anyway you don't like fish do you? You got that from your father. Richard went through a phase where he never ate any type of seafood until he was 14. Then of course I introduced him to the wonders of fried shrimp."

"Oooh, I didn't know that," Jeanne mumbled then went back to eating her burger.

"I never treated Jeanne, my Jeanne right. Times were tough back then, the apartment never made much money and was always in need of repair, the filter on the pool never worked. Every year, without fail, one of the pipes would break. I always regretted installing a pool in the first place. It sure didn't add much value to the place for all the damn maintenance I had to do." Bob took a bite of his fish before continuing.

"Half the tenants never paid their rent on time and I had to personally evict some very scary characters. Anyway by the end of the day I would vent my frustrations on whoever was convenient, usually my wife or my son. Sometimes, more often than I care to admit I let it go too far. I'm not trying to make excuses mind you. I was a pretty awful person back then. I probably still am, how else do you explain the fact that I am the only dirty old millionaire in my social circle without a young goldigger wife?"

He let out a little giggle, took a sip of his water and continued.

"Truth is I treated my wife like a sack of dirt until the day they told me she was dying from cancer. Then I turned my rage towards a boy at the time he needed his father most. Am I sorry? Not a day goes by where I am not full of regret. You probably don't believe me and you certainly won't forgive me, I know I wouldn't if I were in your shoes, but I am sorry and I am utterly amazed to see you all. Especially you Richard, Ricky. It's neither of those anymore is it?"

"Just stick with Ricky. When I went by Ricky, I waited and waited for you to call me that. Now that you are I am going to enjoy it."

After lunch we ended up walking along the harbor so we could talk some more.

"I'm sorry about that comment about letting yourself go Ricky. I don't really think that. You look a bit like I used to. It's sort of unnerving to see yourself in someone you no longer know, I guess," Bob said. "I have done so many interviews where I have had to act hurt over your disappearance, something inside me started to convince me that I truly am mad at you. I'm really not of course. You had to get away from everything, it was the best thing for you."

Robert scanned the harbor for a second then announced "My boat's up ahead would you kids like to see it?"

His boat ended up being the largest yacht in the harbor. The lettering on the back read Where's Ricky with Ventura, California stenciled under it. Seems my grandfather did have a sense of humor after all.

"I'm afraid I can't take you anywhere on it. They took away my license because of my illness, but I haven't had the heart to sell it yet. Would you like it?"

'That's a generous offer, but we have no room for a boat," Dad responded.

Sure we do, I thought. All we need to do would be to decommission another couple of lockers and knock down their internal walls. Too bad I didn't have the guts to vocalize these thoughts.

"Didn't think you would," Bob chuckled. "You know the best thing about owning this boat? I can afford to have someone else do maintenance on it. I don't need to wash it, or check the gas, or tinker with the motor. It's wonderful."

He sat down for a few minutes on one of the couches below deck and went into a coughing jag.

"Sorry about that, my lungs just aren't what they used to be. I never should have taken up smoking. Oh well you can't go back and start over," he said once the coughing subsided.

"I want to leave everything to you guys, but you won't take it, will you Ricky?"

"I can't," Dad said. "I left Ricky behind a long time ago, and I'm never going back, besides the legal mess would be horrendous."

"What about the kids?" Bob asked as we walked back up the stairs towards the deck.

"I have provided for the kids. I'm sure they would love your money, but please don't open up that can of worms. If Steven and Jeanne become famous someday, I want from their own talents and merits, not simply because they are Ricky Stevenson's kids."

"I always thought you would say something like that. So I am going to give it to some foundations for the battered and abused. I may even start one myself and name it for your mother." Bob started to wheeze again and lost his balance. He tumbled into the arms of my father. The two of them said nothing for a few minutes just hugged until Dad said,

"Maybe we should head out, let you get some rest. Do you need a ride?"

"No that's okay, I can call someone to come and get me, I've been staying at my ranch not far from here, If you would ever like to see it you're always invited you know."

"I know."

The rest of us gave Bob a hug before we headed off I glanced back at him as we walked down the harbor. From that vantage point he was just a feeble old man with a cane standing on top of a very large boat waving with all his might.

Chapter 39
Record Shopping with the Stars

When we returned to L.A. later that afternoon it was still too early to go back to the hotel so we decided to explore Melrose Avenue. Dad and I were bored with it after about ten minutes, but Mom and Jeanne wouldn't let us leave. Melrose is filled with vintage clothing stores, so you would have thought I would have been more impressed, but they mostly concentrated on women's clothing. These stores were also ridiculously expensive. $53 for a shirt that was similar to one I bought for five bucks at Highland Thrift? No thank you.

After about an hour of walking in and out of stores with names like Retro Mania or Vintopia, Dad spotted salvation in the form of a large record store. The outside walls were painted with murals of various stars from Hendrix to Elvis to Stevie Ray. Ricky Stevenson was there of course, oddly juxtaposed in between Elvis Costello and Janis Joplin. I assumed that this would be enough to stop my father in his tracks, but he must have had all he could take of looking at vintage go go boots, and seventy five dollar vintage embroidered purses so he promptly announced.

"Steven and I are going in here; you can join us if you want."

Once inside I promptly headed to the oldies sections and to my surprise Dad and Jeanne followed me there. I ignored them and went straight to the S's where they had the Ricky Stevenson and the Sleepers box set displayed prominently. I had wanted the set for ages but I wasn't in the mood to pay seventy eight bucks for a group of CDs, featuring songs I already owned. As I read the blurb on the side of the box Jeanne nudged me.

"I thought Ricky Stevenson's label was Emcee Records, how come this says Rocktime Records on it?" She asked, showing me a new reissue of *The Palmdale Sessions*.

"Emcee was bought out by Rocktime years ago," I told her. "Then Rocktime merged with some big company, I forget which one. It's either that vodka company or the Japanese stereo one. Anyway they just kept the Rocktime name for some of their older records because it's familiar."

"Oh, I was wondering why none of my CD's at home were from Emcee. I guess that explains it." She responded.

As Jeanne put back *The Palmdale Sessions*, I noticed something next to it. *Ricky Stevenson Rarities: Volume Two*. When had this come out? It must have been brand new since I hadn't seen it before, or read any reviews of it in *Major Music Monthly*, or *Guitar Riff*. I picked the CD up and flipped it over. Below the track listing was a brief description of the contents.

From the massive archives of Rocktime Records comes this brand new collection of unreleased cuts by Ricky and the Sleepers. Never before released in CD format and digitally remastered this compilation includes rare B-sides, live tracks, and a song from the never completed Ricky and the Sleepers' Christmas album. Many of these songs have never been available to the general public before. Ricky Stevenson Rarities: Volume Two is a must for any Ricky and the Sleepers fan. Be sure to check out Ricky Stevenson Rarities: Volume One available on Rocktime Records, wherever music is sold. Remember Rocktime: Your number one source for great oldies and new favorites.

I simply had to get this CD. It wasn't something that could wait till we were back home. I looked over and saw Dad next to me looking at another copy of it. After he put it back he turned to me and said.

"You know there is a reason some songs remain unreleased and hidden in vaults, and it's not just to make some greedy record company a pile of money thirty years later. This record has got some truly terrible stuff on it."

"Oh okay, I was just looking at it," I mumbled and put it back. Dad had been in a better mood lately and I didn't want to offend him. I decided I would buy the CD. later.

"Of course I am still going to buy it for you regardless. Consider it a late Christmas present. I haven't heard this stuff in years, maybe it's not as bad as I think," he said and we walked over to the cash register.

The cashier was covered in tattoos and piercings, but he otherwise seemed friendly enough.

"We've been playing the Christmas song off of this on the store sound system," he said. "It's pretty good. Who would have thought Ricky Stevenson would have himself a hit thirty years after he disappeared. You know you look kinda like him."

"Thanks," I started to say but the cashier interrupted me. "No him," he said nodding at Dad. "I could be crazy but you look a little like an older Ricky."

"You are crazy Dan, he looks nothing like Ricky Stevenson," the other cashier, a girl covered in the same amount of piercings said as she slid a CD into a bag. She then turned to my father and said,

"No offense. It's just Dan's a little weird."

"Oh that's okay--none taken. If I really looked like Ricky Stevenson I think more of the ladies in here would have noticed. Don't you?" Dad responded in a joking tone.

Chapter 40
In the Market for Fame

On our last morning in Los Angeles we had time to kill before our flight so Dad took us all driving once again after breakfast. He even played one of my Ricky Stevenson CD's in the car's player and started singing along at key points.

"You don't sound anything like him." Jeanne said.

I disagreed with her after I closed my eyes and listened. I had listened to my Ricky Stevenson CD's and records so many times I had them memorized, and to my ears the voice coming from the front seat could only belong to one person. Sure it was older, and a lot less polished, but he was Ricky no doubt about it.

"You sound like an out of practice Ricky Stevenson to me and I have listened to a lot more Ricky than little-miss-know-it-all." I informed him.

"Well thank you for the compliment Steven, though you should stop putting your sister down. You guys all need to remember it's been a long time. I don't even remember the lyrics to some of the songs," Dad said.

...

We kept on driving until we reached Malibu. Then suddenly my father slowed down and entered a parking lot.

"Wouldn't you know it's still here?" Dad said as he pointed to a chi-chi looking supermarket. He continued his spiel, then got silly about it. "A place of business within the Los Angeles metropolitan area that has been with us since the time I lived here. Amazing! This is an utterly magnificent relic of the mezzo-paleo-Stevensonian era."

"Why are we at a supermarket? We just ate," Mom said dryly. She was clearly unimpressed by Dad's excessive use of words like paleo that he had acquired after our trip to the La Brea tar pits.

"Because," he responded "I used to shop here, and I could really use a candy bar."

Mom gave a deep sigh before she commented. "Jesus Jack It's lucky we had the money from your recording career because the profits from the Stor'N'More would never be enough to satisfy that appetite."

I couldn't tell if Mom was attempting to be funny or if too much of the traffic, crowds, and smog of Los Angeles had made her sarcastic and edgy, but I assumed it was probably the latter. These comments rolled off my father, who was still in a decent mood. So the man liked to eat, was that really such a crime?

"Look I still have the taste of burnt bacon in my mouth and I just want a mint or something. Don't you want to see the supermarket that once met the shopping needs of Ricky Stevenson, the world's most famous missing man? Was it something located within these very walls that made him run? Could the wrong brand of macaroni have set him off? Come on."

The supermarket didn't just look glitzy from the outside. Once we stepped inside we were inundated by what seemed like hundreds of market employees offering us free samples of crazy hors'd'ouvres. I wondered how many of these ended up getting spilled onto the marble floors and if you did spill would one of those smiling people with the push brooms would show up like they did at Disneyland. Soft music wafted around us and we turned and saw an actual baby grand piano being softly played near the floral department.

"Talk about overkill, I bet your candy bar is going to end up costing ten dollars," Mom said, as she took all of this in.

"It didn't look anything like this thirty years ago," Dad told her. When I shopped here it was a regular supermarket. I guess to stay in business in Los Angeles for this long you have to become a tourist destination. Now come on, I have got to see the rest of this place."

We slowly wandered the aisles with Mom feigning shock at the high prices, Jeanne constantly scanning for celebrities, and me and Dad looking at all the weird yuppie brands of stuff they carried.

They even had an entire health food section full of displays and signs that went something like this: We proudly feature *Dr. Healthbody's:* tofu based, soy enhanced, macrobiotic skim babyfood. *Dr. Healthbody's* is the easiest way to guarantee your kid will hate you from the very start. Be sure to check out our line of organic pet foods so Fido will resent you too.

"Ewww. That is so disgusting," Jeanne said pointing at something, after we had left the granola section and ventured towards the meats.

We all looked up and saw what appeared to be huge sides of beef hanging up in a glass case behind the meat department.

"Did you think meat just always comes in those little cellophane packages?" Dad asked her.

"No but that is just gross, I am so going to become a vegetarian," Jeanne announced.

I wondered if that meant she would start eating food from *Dr. Healthbody's* line of frozen dinners for adolescents.

"You say that now, but just wait till you're hungry again," Dad told her just before she and Mom wandered off to explore more departments.

Once we reached the cereal aisle Dad mulled over buying a symbolic box of Cheerios but decided not to, once he saw how much they charged. Instead he grabbed a box of Rice Krispies and pretended to be fascinated by the Snap, Crackle and Pop maze on the back. Then he glanced from side to side, and when he was satisfied no one was looking he pulled a marking pen from his pants' pocket and quickly scrawled something on the box. Before he put it back on the shelf behind some other boxes Dad let me read what he had written.

This is the last time I will ever do this--Ricky Stevenson.

What amazed me was the fact that after all these years he could still scrawl one of the world's most famous signatures with perfection. Someone was certainly going to get a surprise alongside their milk at breakfast.

We reunited with Jeanne and Mom in the deli department, which appeared to be the most bustling section in the whole store.

"Check out those annoying preppies, they are totally about to jump all over that poor guy who looks just like Johnny Candell," Jeanne said, slightly nodding towards the cheeses, her glasses falling down her nose as usual.

I tried not to chuckle at the fact that math contest winning, straight A's getting Jeanne actually classified other people as preppy.

"Maybe that really is Johnny Candell," I told her.

"Yeah maybe, shut up I want to see this," she said.

There were two teenage girls standing in front of the normal brands of cheese giggling and eyeing a father and his two kids looking at the fancier varieties. I could just tell those girls were the ultra-annoying loud giggly type. While they were busy oozing obnoxiousness, I pictured them in Delacourte. They would be right at home on our cheerleading team, but they didn't seem the type to shop at a place like this. For all I know their fathers were studio heads or something. We pretended to be looking at some meat and cheese trays while we watched them pounce on the poor unsuspecting dad.

"Oh my God are you, like, Johnny Candell?" One of them said in a loud whisper.

"Uh no I'm afraid you are mistaken" He said. Though he tried to muffle his words and speak in a mumble, it wasn't enough to stop him from sounding exactly like the lead singer of Generation Lies.

For a few moments I forgot all of my father's horror stories about fame. Johnny Candell--the Johnny Candell--was standing almost directly in front of me. If I got his autograph for Dave, my best friend would probably be at my beck and call for the rest of his natural life. No wait, what if I got a signature for all of my friends, then I could brag to the popular kids about how I had hung out with Johnny on my trip to LA. No--If I got a picture of myself with Johnny Candell...

"Yeah you are. We can like totally tell," One of the cheerleaders loudly said, interrupting my train of delusional thought.

"I love your new album," the other told him.

"Can I have your autograph?"

"Look kids I'm just trying to shop for my kid's birthday so don't make a big deal out of this okay," Johnny said, as he signed an oat bran box, his eyes sweeping back and forth.

Johnny's desperate plea was ignored when the other girl spotted another friend across the store.

"Oh my God Jenny-Jenny look! Johnny Candell is totally signing his autograph for me!"

Johnny quickly signed the other girl's box and mumbled "Come on kids let's go." but by then it was too late.

Other people were suddenly turning their heads and making their way towards the deli department. Even some of the shoppers who looked more well-heeled were kissing up to Johnny.

"Great show last year at The Garden, It was totally worth flying to New York for," announced one man wearing all black, while an older designer clad woman passed a notebook from the stationary department over the crowd and announced:

"My granddaughter just adores you."

Johnny's head was swiveling back and forth and he leaned to the side looking for a way out all while maintaining a death grip on each of his children. Finally an older gentleman stepped in front of his cart and said

"You people should all be ashamed. This young man is simply trying to get some supplies for his child's party."

The two girls who had started the commotion in the first place started giggling again. This time they were approaching Johnny's unlikely savior.

"Oh my god you are on that show *Ultimate Law!* My mom totally watches that. Can I have your autograph for her?" she squealed.

As the pandemonium grew worse we left the deli department to purchase Dad's candy bar while the lines were short. Unfortunately it seemed most of the checkers had left their posts to see what all the commotion was about leaving just one checker and bagger to deal with a huge line. We decided to forgo the candy purchase and as we left we could hear snippets of the remaining cashier and bagger's gripes.

"They are like totally breaking the respect and privacy rule. I hope they all get fired."

"Yeah, but come on, it's Johnny Candell. I sure hope Gillian gets me an autograph like she promised."

"If I gave him my demo tape--do you think he would listen?"

...

We stepped outside and once inside the car, Dad turned toward Jeanne and me.

"Now do you believe me when I say fame is not all it's cracked up to be?"

"Yeah, I believe you," I said.

"I don't know about you guys but I am definitely ready to go home now," he said.

I returned Dad's gaze and responded. "I couldn't agree with you more."

I had no idea what would happen once we returned home to Delacourte. I thought about the flyer for Dexter Community College that I had never bothered to take out of my backpack. Maybe sticking close to home after high school wasn't such a bad idea after all.

It's not like I could go back in time, and not open locker seventeen. Not that I had any regrets about learning the truth. Solving the mystery of what happened to Ricky Stevenson had changed me. Friends and family, those are the important things in life. Not the superficial. I didn't need a huge mansion, and a pool with girls everywhere. Well okay, I did need some of the girls, and a larger house would be nice, and a pool would be nice, but I don't need one. Unless it has that new girl from *Baywatch*, lounging next to the diving board.

Once I got home, life was going to be different. I know it's going to be hard keeping the secret from everyone at school, I know it's going to be hard to concentrate on school enough to graduate with a halfway decent G.P.A., and I know it's going to be difficult to figure out what career I should go into, especially now that Ricky Stevenson tribute artist is no longer an option. I don't know what else the future holds but I know I can handle it. I can handle anything now that I know there is rock'n'roll in locker seventeen.

The End

ABOUT THE AUTHOR

Shannon Brown currently runs www.tshirtfort.com a funny online t-shirt and gift website, She holds a B.A. in communications from Chico State University. Shannon lives in the Bay Area.

For more information about this book and upcoming projects please visit www.locker17.com

15445355R00137

Made in the USA
Lexington, KY
28 May 2012